Two Spirit Ranch

A Romance

by
Jaime Stryker

Chances at Romance
www.chancesatromance.com
A Chances Press, LLC imprint

Two Spirit Ranch: A Romance

For Crystal L.,
You have inspired me in more
ways than you'll know.

Copyright 2012 by Jaime Stryker

Published by Chances Press, LLC,

Las Vegas, NV

For more on Jaime Stryker, please visit

www.chancesatromance.com.

Prologue

For some odd reason, Terri had always noticed the little things when her life seemingly had begun to spiral out of control. Tonight, for one, it was the vastness of the summer Montana night sky. The stars twinkled in a way they never could in the artificial light drenched Manhattan skies. Here, in "Big Sky Country," the stars appeared to stretch out forever bathing the night in what should be an intoxicatingly romantic sight. The grasshoppers chirped quietly in the background, and a slight crisp breeze blew through the air, ruffling her soft sun yellow skirt and the caramel colored curls that highlighted her face.

She remembered how her Uncle Bud had described his Montana ranch home as a slice of heaven you can't buy in any store—even in New York City. Terri had thought him to be crazy for leaving the bustling, opportunity-filled life of the Big Apple for one smack in the middle of what amounted to little more than a village.

"Sometimes you just need to shake things up, do the unexpected, and challenge yourself," Uncle Bud had said at their tearful goodbye before giving a teenage Terri a big hug and hopping into his over packed VW Beetle.

Now older and the proverbial wiser, she had a better idea of what he meant, but now she feared it might be too late for her just when she'd finally...

"Terri, aren't you going to say something?" she heard Jake say as he stood behind her.

Handsome, wonderful Jake. She could smell his clean masculine scent wafting through the air, and without needing to turn around she could see his fit, muscular form in his sheriff's office uniform. Strong, sensitive Jake. She should have been honest with him right at the get-go. But it had been the fear of this moment right here that had her act against her better judgment, her lawyer instincts of laying out the evidence right at the beginning. No surprises later. Let the jury know what's at hand from the start. That's the way you win people over.

But she had never intended to *want* to win anybody over in this small town. She only wanted to get away from her life in the Big Apple and to feel closer to her Uncle Bud after his passing. She never imagined she would get wrapped up into life here...let alone into *someone* here.

Finally, she turned around to face Jake, eye to eye, just as she did the jurors in all of her cases. She'd lay out the case for why she felt, whether it had been right or wrong, to keep silent about her past. She kept quiet, even though she could look into his deep chestnut brown eyes and see this relationship obviously went beyond the point of anything casual for Jake, which is what made this so hard, so messy and so emotional.

Even though she had gotten the chance to know him, *to see him*, over the past few days, the mere sight of him still took her breath away as no man ever did before. Over six foot three inches tall and built of a solid wall of muscle, Jake had a commanding presence. But one look in his eyes and she saw him as the protector he was. He took the ethics and oath of his sheriff's badge seriously. His midnight dark wavy hair and eternal five o'clock shadow just added to an already smoldering specimen of masculinity. And this man stood before her waiting for a response from her.

"Your cousin, Carl, spoke to you didn't he?" she said at last breaking the silence, averting her eyes, feeling vulnerable under his steely gaze. "You know, don't you?"

"I do," Jake said, holding his uniform hat by his side, forever the perfect gentleman even when he perhaps had a good reason not to be anymore. "What I want to know is why *you* didn't tell me? You had every chance. Do you know how it felt to have Carl be the one to tell me?"

Jake paused, and he appeared to be struggling for the words to express himself. She knew he had never been in quite the same situation before, not out here in small town Montana. She had learned to give people time to process things when needed which had been something she had never been good at in her younger years. If people didn't accept her, Terri simply moved on. But this was different. He was different, or so she thought. She didn't want to run away from him. Her instinct was quite the opposite. She wanted him to hold her in his strong arms and protect her even more. But she wasn't sure how he felt about the situation, about her.

"How did it make you feel?" she asked, the words barely escaping her throat.

"Betrayed," he said finally, the words cutting into her heart like a sharp knife into butter. "I don't pretend to understand everything...*yet*. I may be a small town sheriff but didn't you respect me enough to tell the truth? But I would have rather heard it from you first hand. Don't you think I deserved at least that, Terri? Don't you? Didn't I deserve some respect after all we've been through?"

"You do," she admitted. ""I don't know how I could have handled anything here without you, Jake. I needed you. I was afraid..."

"Of?"

"What do you mean *of?*" she said, suddenly sounding defensive. "You must know how it scared me to tell you...especially after we...made love. You must know how it scared me to tell you. But then I wanted to tell you the next morning...but you were gone. I felt so abandoned."

Jake felt a twinge of guilt upon hearing the word *abandoned*.

"I just never thought things would go this far, Jake," she admitted. "And last night happened. It was special to me. I don't know how you feel but I'll always remember it…"

"Well, the jury's still out," he said, searching for additional words to adequately express how he felt. "I'm not sure where all this is going. But here we are."

She took a deep breath and asked the one question she feared knowing the answer to the most, "Does knowing everything change the way you feel?"

He turned to face her, his dark eyes an enigma, and Terri searched his countenance for the answer that would change her life forever.

Chapter 1

"Terri, the client's waiting in to the conference room. Are you ready?" Martin, a senior partner at her firm, said after poking his head into her office.

Startled, Terri, wearing a smart navy Prada pantsuit, swiveled her chair around from her window with its view of Central Park. She had been staring outside of it for the past fifteen minutes which was very unlike her, but her mind had been sent reeling trying to process the call she had received just twenty minutes earlier. She always seemed too busy and focused to enjoy the view.

"Yes, I'm ready. I'm sorry, Martin. My mind is just a little scattered today."

She began to shuffle some papers around on her desk and looked for her notes on the McBriar case, a software company suing another one over copyright infringement.

"By the way," Martin said, all smiles as he walked up to her desk and laid a newspaper across it. "You trying to make us feel bad with all of your *pro bono* work on top of the regular eighty hour work week? Geez, Terri!"

The newspaper article. She had forgotten all about it in the middle of the day's hectic schedule. The reporter had told her it would be in today's edition, and she meant to grab a few copies at the newsstand next to her loft. She had woken up late, something else that had been unlike her, and rushed off to work forgetting all about it. Maybe she was overextending herself, but the work discussed in the article felt more important than anything else in her career up to that point especially compared with an impersonal lawsuit from a software giant.

"You saw the article!" Terri exclaimed, feeling a sense of pride and momentarily forgetting her sadness.

"The whole firm is talking about it," Martin said, sitting in one of the overstuffed leather chairs facing her desk. Martin was a jovial man in his late fifties, slightly chubby, ruddy cheeks, with a deep laugh that would make Santa Claus jealous. He had also been one of Terri's biggest cheerleaders the past few years.

"The other senior partners," Martin continued, "if pressed on the issue, are tickled pink about the publicity this has brought the firm in regards to being *diversity friendly.* You did good, kid!"

"Thanks, Martin," Terri said, starting to feel choked up emotions overwhelming her for once.

"Don't mention it," Martin said, waving his hand dismissively.

"No, I mean it. You've done so much always standing by me," Terri said, and at that moment, she couldn't hold it in anymore. The tears began to flow, and poor Martin, unused to seeing normally composed Terri act so emotional appeared shocked and unsure what to do next. "I couldn't have asked for a better friend here at work."

"Hey, hey! You okay? What's going on?"

"The client. We need to get going," Terri said, trying to internally command the tears to stop as she finished sorting her notes.

Martin looked behind him and through the open door to her office. He got up, shut the door, and sat back down. "Screw the client for once. Tell me what's going on. We're friends here."

Terri took a deep breath to try and steady her nerves while looking into Martin's trustworthy face before talking.

"I got a phone call from Montana not too long ago. My Uncle Bud passed unexpectedly. Heart attack. Christ, they already had the funeral and no one in my family bothered to even call me to tell me. Not that they call any other time, either. But this...I don't understand. They know how close Uncle Bud and I always were. He was always so supportive of me. *Like you.*"

"Ah, jeez, Terri. I'm so sorry to hear about your loss. I don't know what to say. I can't believe your family wouldn't tell you."

"You won't believe what he did before he passed though," she said, shaking her head still not believing it herself.

"What?"

"He left me his ranch in Montana. It was the only thing he owned out right. Can you imagine me hanging out at a ranch in Montana?"

she said, trying to force out a little chuckle to lighten the mood. That's how she always had been. She tried to make others comfortable more than herself. She wished she could move past that, but it had become so ingrained in her from before.

"Why don't you take some time and go out there?" Martin suggested.

Terri shook her head and motioned to all the files on her desk.

"I can't," she said immediately dismissing the idea. "There's too much work to be done."

"Look. You more than deserve it. Trust me. Take some personal time. Don't try and work through it like I did. That's how you end up in the hospital at forty-five with a heart attack. Besides, you might meet some nice cowboy up there and poor Tom will get the heave-ho...."

"Martin!" She sighed loudly yet smiled slightly. Martin was always the joker around the office even in the tensest moments.

"Seriously. Think about it," Martin said. He picked up the newspaper, read over the headline again, and said, "And this is something truly to be proud of. This is the important stuff in life. Don't ever forget it."

After a sweltering hot day at the office, the evening cooled down quite nicely. The taxi gods must have been smiling since she arrived twenty minutes early at the restaurant and was promptly seated. Her boyfriend, Tom, had called her earlier in the day and wanted "to talk" and after the day she had had, she certainly needed to lean on him for some support. She decided she wouldn't mention the news about her Uncle Bud until seeing him in person.

She didn't want to jump to any conclusions, but she wondered if he might pop the question. Things had been getting pretty serious lately after they met at a legal conference a year ago. She and Tom had been almost inseparable ever since, and he had taken her to numerous functions at his law firm. If that wasn't a sign of being serious, what was?

She had taken extra care in dressing for dinner. She wore her new black Escada dress, the pearl and diamond earrings Tom had given her for Christmas, and her new Jimmy Choo heels. No matter how bad of a day she had, Tom had a calming effect and would always bring a smile to her face. She sure needed that now.

At her apartment earlier, while digging in the back of a drawer for a bangle bracelet, she paused when she came across a picture of another man, the one she had tried to put behind her. *Him.* The man, surrounded by some friends from law school, smiled in the picture, but Terri could recognize the hurt in his eyes. She didn't keep pictures of *him* around, as it was still a little too painful, to relive the memories. However, she had hung on to this picture because it was taken not long before she had the greatest revelation of her life.

The waiter at the restaurant asked if she'd like to order a drink while she waited, and she ordered a glass of merlot. She glanced at her watch and noticed that Tom was running late which was very unlike him. She hoped his taxi hadn't gotten caught in the snarling Big Apple traffic. He would always leave a voicemail or sent a text if he was late—the consummate professional. She needed to kiss him and hold his hand for reassurance.

Tom. He had chestnut brown hair and maintained his husky physique by playing rugby on weekends. It was fireworks between them from the get go. She felt an intense passion that she had never encountered before. Tom also had proven one of her deepest fears that she harbored to be false--that she wouldn't find a man who loved her for exactly who she was. In fact, they had made love earlier that morning and she was finally, truly, letting herself be open and vulnerable to this man, after so many hardships getting to where she was.

"Hi," Tom's deep voice came from behind her as his strong hand briefly touched her lithe shoulder. She always liked his touch—firm and confident, yet soft and tender. He smiled. Damn, he had a cute smile. And he wore his Armani suit, not the other way around.

The waiter dropped off a bottle of Chateau Margaux. Their usual. Sometimes the usual was quite comforting. Humans like predictability a professor once told her.

"How are you, sweetie?" she asked,

reaching across the table and placing her hand on top of his.

"Fine," he answered, sounding a little short. "How are you?"

"It's been a crazy day," she said, readying herself to tell him the news about Uncle Bud, but before she could the waiter appeared and poured them each a glass of the Chateau Margaux. Tom startled her by practically guzzling down his glass and then telling the waiter they'd need a few minutes to decide on dinner.

"Are you okay, Tom?" she asked momentarily forgetting about her own troubles and feeling worried about him. He seemed different in a way tonight. She couldn't quite place it. It was a certain look in is eyes. He was there and not there at the same time. The more she thought about it he had been a little distant the past few days, not as talkative, a little more reserved. Terri bit into one of the warm bread rolls dipped into balsamic vinegar and olive oil when Tom spoke.

He looked at her earnestly with a puzzling expression that was unfamiliar to Terri. He inhaled and paused before speaking. "Terri, I just wanted to tell you that I'm really fond of you and I respect you, but I'm going to have to let you go. If I'm going to move up in the firm, I don't think having a girlfriend, um, like you would be acceptable to the partners."

"*Like me*? What do you mean? You're dumping me?" Terri asked incredulously, almost choking on the bread in her throat.

14

"People at the office have been..." he said, glancing around the room as if they may be spied on.

"Have been what, Tom?" she said, her stomach turned into knots and the wine suddenly tasted like vinegar.

"Talking. After the newspaper article today, some of the partners at the firm recognized your picture and..."

Terri could feel her face flush with anger. After all this time, now her background was suddenly an issue for him.

"So, you're embarrassed by having a girlfriend who's transgendered?" she finally said, the words almost getting stuck in her throat. "I was honest from you from the very beginning, and you said you didn't have a problem with it."

She watched Tom fidget in his seat.

"I'm giving you your freedom," Tom said, looking at her, while her eyes reddened. "We've had a wonderful year, but I'm ready to move on. I might run for office someday and though people are more open minded here in New York, I don't think someone like you would be...accepted in America's heartland."

"You're dumping me of what Midwesterners might think? Because an article about my *pro bono* work for the Transgendered Community Center of New York appeared in the paper?" she asked. "Or is it because you're not man enough to be honest with people about who you've been dating?"

"Please, lower your voice, Terri. People

are staring," Tom hushed her, his eyes scanning the crowded restaurant. "Listen, I had a great time. The sex was great. Awesome, actually."

His words reducing their whole relationship to *sex* felt like a knife in her heart. She sucked in her breath for a moment and tried to steady herself. She met a lot of men who wanted to treat her like an object, but not a person. To satisfy some fetish. This *couldn't* be happening. How could she have possibly read the entire situation so wrong?

"You are a beautiful person, inside and out, but I have to think about my future...," Tom said, his voice trailing off.

"Stop!" she said, interrupting him in midsentence. "I can't believe you're doing this to me. I thought we were serious and maybe, just maybe, I thought we were headed towards marriage. You told me over and over that the fact I was born in the wrong body made no difference to you!"

Tom stared down at his lap avoiding her eyes, but she began to notice that others in the restaurant were now paying attention to the scene. She hadn't realized how loud her voice had become in anger.

"I'm sorry, Terri. Sometimes things change. Life is unpredictable sometimes," Tom said meekly and still staring down into his lap.

"Things change," Terri muttered. "That's all you can say? I feel like I never even knew you. Now I know what kind of man you really are, Tom. Thank you. "

"So, are we ready to order?" the waiter asked, appearing out of nowhere and seemingly oblivious to the unfolding drama.

"I think we're through here," Terri said, standing up and tossing her cloth napkin on the table. "The *gentleman* will get the bill."

She marched out of the restaurant not looking back but unable now to hold back the torrent of tears as they streamed down her face. The two people she thought she could count on in this world, her uncle and her boyfriend, had been snapped away from her in one quick day. Two people she loved.

Terri vainly tried to hail a cab as a sudden summer rain started permeating the air. Unable to get a taxi, Terri just ran down the street not sure where she was going, just wanting to go, go anywhere, to vainly escape the feelings inside of her. She just ran, focusing on her breath and the pain in her feet. She didn't notice people on the sidewalk stopping to stare at this obviously upset woman racing down the street. She was so unaware; she didn't notice the rain mixed with the tears streaming down her face.

Terri kept running. For two weeks, she dove into her work at the law firm and the community center just keeping busy, trying to forget.

Finally, when Martin caught her in her office one afternoon, her back to the door, and crying he placed a hand on her shoulder and said,

"Terri, maybe you really should take that leave of absence. It would do you good. You've been through a lot."

She nodded in agreement. How could she expect to take care of clients, both the paying ones and her work at the community center, if she didn't take care of herself?

"Maybe I should take a little time. Maybe go to my uncle's ranch in Montana and decide what to do with the property."

"I think that sounds like a perfect idea. I'll smooth over the request with the other partners. Don't worry about it. Maybe you need a change of scenery to give you a new perspective on things."

"Thank you, Martin," Terri said, already feeling a little better at the thought of putting some space between herself and Manhattan.

Three days later, Terri flew to Billings, Montana. She rented a car and headed to the small town where Uncle Bud had moved to. It was such a blur; she didn't notice she was speeding down the highway past the sign that read "Clearview, Montana, population 797."

She tried vainly to hold back the continuing thoughts of Tom and her heartbreak while driving. She cranked up the stereo and played her favorite Bon Jovi CDs from the 80s and drove her Mini Cooper rental down the seemingly endless Montana road. But it was to no avail. This particular stretch of road out of

Billings was long and flat, so her mind wandered back to the reason for her escape. Escape. An escape from her memories. An escape from New York. And especially an escape from herself. But then she remembered that she knew better than anyone there was no way anyone could out run their own self. Sooner or later, you had to face that reflection in the mirror and its truth.

Sheriff Jake Collins was enjoying another peaceful day in Clearview, Montana, a small town outside of Billings. Though he lived in Montana all his life, the area's beauty never ceased to amaze him. The land was timeless and yet alive with history. He didn't understand why his cousin Carl wanted to erase all this natural beauty with his huge condo and planned community development proposal. When Jake went to the big city, all he could remember were the generic box stores and main streets lined with chain restaurants and antsy teenagers having parking lot parties. He didn't want Clearview turned into that. Here people still all knew each other, and there was a real community. It was a simpler life and slower pace but there are some things of value you can't put a price tag on.

Suddenly, he clocked a little Mini Cooper whizzing by erratically and going fifteen miles over the speed limit.

"What the…? Uh, oh. Time to earn your paycheck today, Jake," he muttered to himself turning on the siren and following the car into

town. "Not on my watch, you don't, buddy."
The siren's wail pierced the dry air and dissipated into the vast Yellowstone Valley.

Terri awoke from her reverie. She looked at her rearview mirror and wiped away the tears from her reddened eyes.
Oh, no, she thought. *Just what I needed.* Bad things always happen in threes. First Uncle Bud. Then Tom. And now being pursued by a sheriff's patrol car. She pulled over, trying to regain her composure. All she could see were the flashing lights in the rear view mirror, obscuring her view of the officer wearing intimidating mirrored sunglasses steadily approaching her rental.

Nice body she thought to herself. For a country guy. He certainly filled out his officer's uniform quite well.

He had dark hair and a handsomeness like the silver screen stars of the past. He looked comfortable in his skin which, to Terri, was quite intriguing.

"License and registration, please," said the officer. Terri eyed his name tag, "COLLINS." His voice was pure country--deep, slow and deliberate.

"I'm sorry, Officer...er, Collins. I'm sorry, is my taillight out?" she asked, smiling coyly while opening her Coach wallet to hand over the license.

"No ma'am. Just speeding down the road

like a bat out of hell, and it's sheriff. Sheriff Collins." He looked at her driver's license photo and then at her. It wasn't a bad photo. She worked the Department of Motor Vehicles employee to take a few extra shots during a slow shift to increase her chance of a cute photo.

"Well, Miss Lawson, you sure are long ways from New York but 'round these parts there is a thing called the speed limit," the sheriff said while handing back the license.

"Sorry, Sheriff. It won't happen again. I don't want to bore you, but it's been a *really* rough few weeks for me," she said, sighing audibly.

"Well, I'm sorry things aren't going your way, ma'am, but the speed limit is the same on good days and bad ones." Jake said. He'd heard every sob story in the book during his years of pulling people over. "We have a saying 'round these parts. 'If you get thrown from a horse, you have to get up and get back on, unless you landed on a cactus…'"

"And then what happens?" Terri asked, bemused at the imagery despite herself.

"Well, then you have to roll around and scream in pain," the sheriff smiled while Terri rolled her eyes. "But all kidding aside, please obey the speed limits."

"Okay, sir. I'm sorry."

Jake looked down at the ground and kicked a little dirt off his shoes. He usually did not hesitate. By now, the ticket book should be out, and his pen scribbling furiously. Instead, he found himself enchanted by this woman's smile. She was a helluva looker that was for sure. In her fancy clothes, she was the perfect image of a city lady. He wondered what had brought her to these parts. He had caught the rental car plates on the vehicle earlier. Rarely, did he ever come across someone so strikingly beautiful on this stretch of highway.

"If you promise to slow down, maybe I can let you go with a warning."

She gave him that dazzling smile again, the kind Jake thought could light up a whole room, and said, "Oh, my goodness. Thank you so much, Sheriff. I promise to slow down. Cross my heart."

She even made the little hand gesture across her chest, and Jake couldn't help but chuckle.

"You're welcome" he replied, catching just the slightest glimpse of cleavage and feeling a little embarrassed about it like a schoolboy.

"May I ask your name?" she asked.

"Jake. Jake Collins. Sherriff of Clearwater," he said proudly.

"Nice to meet you, Jake. I'm Terri." She held out her French manicured hand to the Jake, which he shook firmly.

"Where are you headed to, Miss Terri?" he asked.

"Oh, just Terri, please. My Uncle Bud moved out here and bought a ranch years ago. He passed away, and now I'm handling his estate," she said, a tear coming to her eye thinking about him.

"Oh, you must mean Bud Harley? We all know each other around these parts. I'm sorry for your loss, Miss Lawson. I knew your uncle well. Good man. I actually worked for him a couple of summers during high school. Funny, he never mentioned a niece…," he said.

Terri quickly changed the subject. "Um, I've had a long day, and I'm desperate to get to the powder room. Can you tell me the quickest way to get to the ranch house? Again, I'm sorry for speeding. I didn't mean to harm anyone," Terry confessed.

"Actually, it'd be easier if you followed me. The roads can be a bit confusing for the uninitiated. Do you mind a police escort?" Jake asked.

With everything from the past two weeks, Terri was open for anything. "Oh, alright. Why not?" She was beginning to understand why her Uncle Bud loved Montana so much.

Chapter 2

Terri dutifully followed the sheriff's car down meandering roads with hardly any signage. The sun was setting and she said a silent prayer. She easily imagined how it could've turned out differently if she had gotten lost on these desolate roads. Stranded. No gas. Lost. Looking crazy. Eaten by coyotes. That's how her city mind worked sometimes. And her mind was also on the fine man in front of her. Sheriff Jake Collins was a hottie, she thought. But if she learned anything from her relationship from Tom was that heartbreak can come in handsome packages.

Thankfully, the sheriff led her directly to the driveway of the home of her late Uncle Bud.

The ranch turned out not to be what she had expected, but then she wasn't sure what she had expected to begin with. Maybe a rustic looking cabin surrounded by a lot of thick patches of trees and fields. Instead, she found a brightly blue colored home, nicely kept, with immaculate flower gardens in front. She never took her Uncle Bud for the flower planting type.

She got out of her car as did the dapper sheriff in his uniform, who looked good enough to eat, or at least lick all over, and Terri *did not* have the usual weakness for men in uniform.

"Well, this is where I leave you, Terri."

"Thanks, Sherriff," she said.

He took off his hat and held it against his chest.

"You can call me, Jake," he replied.

"Thank you, *Jake*."

She couldn't help but feel a stirring of attraction for this gallant man.

"Perhaps I'll see you around again while I'm here," she added.

"It's a small town. We'll see each other. I'm sure. Just go over to Clearwater Café. It's where most of the town spends their free time. You must know of Sally."

"Sally?" she asked, perplexed. "I don't believe so."

"Oh, I'm sorry. Again, small town. We assume everyone knows of everyone and with your uncle having lived here. Bud and Sally, who owns the cafe, were a bit of...an item the past year. She spent a good amount of time out here. If you have any questions about the property she can probably answer them."

That explained the flower garden, Terri thought. She couldn't believe she had never heard that Uncle Bud had been dating someone, but then she'd been so busy the past year she didn't do a good job of keeping in touch she sadly realized.

"Well, thanks again. I'll be sure to check out the cafe and meet Sally, too."

"Yes, m'am," Jake said, placing his hat back on his head. "Take care now."

She noticed that he appeared a little

hesitant to leave, and she wondered if maybe...just maybe...he felt the same kind of attraction she did. But then she reminded herself that after everything from the past couple of weeks, all she came here to do was clear her head and decide what to do with Uncle Bud's house. Why complicate things?

"You, too. Have a great evening," she told him.

He nodded and with that he got back in his patrol car and drove off.

She decided to come back later and get her luggage. Instead, she took the key Uncle Bud's lawyer had sent to her and went up to the house which was surrounded by lovely quiet acres of land. It was a two story wooden building with lovely detailing outside down to the white picket fence, surrounded by the flat lands but which were then circled by numerous mountain ranges. In the dim light, she could see a few cattle were grazing in the distance.

She walked up the creaky wooden steps up to the door. She inserted the key and threw open the door to the dark quiet home. The house still smelled of Uncle Bud. She ventured into the nearby living room with its rustic sofa and chair. Family pictures were scattered over the fireplace mantle, and she found a picture of herself in Central Park during a visit from her uncle not taken long after she transitioned. She positively beamed in the picture radiating happiness and a sense of self-acceptance she never had before, and it warmed her heart to see that he had framed it. When she turned around she noticed on the opposite wall still hung a picture of *him*, Terrence. It was the same picture she had found in her bedroom drawer the night she went to meet Tom. He had kept this picture up, too.

It always startled her a bit to see a picture of her former self. The body she had lived in then had always felt like a stranger's from as far back as she remembered. Looking at it now, the person seemed like a distant memory. Almost like the feeling of waking after a long dream. On a conscious level, she knew that was her in the photo, but it felt so unreal since she never identified with the person in that body. In fact, going through puberty was very difficult. Imagine the shock of seeing your girl friends grow breasts and wider hips while you were getting hairier and your voice started to deepen. It was feeling like an unwelcome stranger in her own body and jealous that your friends were turning into young women while you were becoming what felt like a foreigner, a deceiver. Only after years of therapy did "he," Terrence, realize he was born in the wrong body.

Uncle Bud had been the only one in her family who supported her transition. A leftover hippie from the 1960s and 70s, he believed in the individual's freedom and dignity. At one low point, he mentioned the Native American "two spirit people" he had learned of since living in Montana, individuals of the tribe who assumed the identity of the opposite gender.

"They were two-spirits and were

respected by the tribe," Uncle Bud told her during an emotional phone conversation when Terrence Lawson confessed "he" could no longer live in the body "he" possessed. That conversation gave her some of the strength to move on with the decision. First, she started to wear women's clothes and eventually assumed a new identity, legal name change and all. It was hard at first just becoming used to the fact that she could be true to herself that she didn't have to put on a front of being a man when she didn't feel the least bit like a man inside. The pain of the surgery had been the worst she had ever felt in her life. But looking back, the pain was the birth of the person she was always meant to be.

The sudden ring of the doorbell startled her and brought her back to the present. She couldn't imagine who could be dropping by here in the middle of nowhere when she knew no one unless it could be the sheriff again. *Now that would be a pleasant surprise,* she thought. She began to be aware of a warmness that permeated her body thinking about Sheriff Jake, which surprised her since her wounds from Tom were so fresh. Maybe Jake was right about getting back up on the horse...

She looked through the peephole and saw a dark blonde haired man at the front door wearing a brown business suit and yellow tie. He sure didn't look like he fit in around the area, Terri thought. He looked like a city businessman. And even more eerie was his slight resemblance to the sheriff, but the two men carried themselves in completely different ways.

She cracked open the door and said, "Yes? May I help you?"

"Good day, ma'am. My name's Carl Collins. I work for the Clearview Estates Resort housing development over the hill there," the man said handing her a business card. Something about him reminded her of an unsavory used car salesman trying to pawn a lemon off on someone. "Word through the grapevine was that a relative of Bud's would be visiting soon, and I just happened to drive by and see a car here."

"Well, news does travel fast around here, doesn't it, Mr. Collins?" she said, opening the door a little wider. "I'm Terri. Terri Lawson. Bud's niece."

He flashed a big toothy grin and continued, "Pleasure to meet you ma'am. I just wanted to welcome you to town and that if you ever need anything, please do not hesitate to ask.

"Why thank you, Mr. Collins."

"You can call me Carl. The development I represent is looking to expand its golf course and housing units and this is a prime location for development. If you feel like selling your property…"

She eyed him suspiciously and then said, "I haven't given much thought to it as I just got into town. Is everyone in this town named Collins? I just met a Sheriff Collins…"

"Ah, you must have met Jake. That boy is my cousin, ma'am. Hope he didn't give you a ticket. He's a stickler for speed limits."

"Your cousin was very gracious, Mr. Collins."

"Perhaps I could set up a meeting with the rest of the development group. You could find out what we're offering..."

"I'm sorry Mr. Collins. I don't think I'm interested right now. My uncle only just passed away, and I'm just trying to process that. I...uh...appreciate your stopping by though," Terri said while trying to shut the door.

Carl put out his hand, gently but firmly, preventing the door from being shut. "I feel your loss, Miss Lawson. Your uncle was an upstanding member of this community, a fine, fine man, and his passing was truly a sad occasion." He cleared his throat and looked at her again. "However, I do know he did leave a lot of unpaid bills including back property taxes. My company is willing to pay the bills and offer a nice monetary package that would meet your satisfaction for everyone's benefit," he said nodding with a smile.

What a salesman, Terri thought. "Thank you for letting me know, Mr. Collins. But I don't think I am going to sell right now."

She noticed his face momentarily harden before breaking out into another smile. "I understand this may a troubling time for your family. Thank you for your time. When...err, if you change your mind, please let me know. Here's my card," he said thrusting it towards her.

"Thank you," she said, taking the card

and trying to convey her lack of enthusiasm. She had only just arrived. The last thing she could think about this moment was selling her last connection to her uncle.

Carl, undeterred, continued, "I truly believe development of Clearview is the key to this area's future success. It's been a pleasure." With that he walked over to his car and sped off.

She closed the door behind her, and realized that the man's presence had sent an uneasy chill through her body. As a lawyer, Terri had developed a sixth sense in knowing when others were hiding ulterior motives, and Carl Collins reeked of it.

As Carl drove off, he thought to himself, *I think there are ways to make you change your mind, Miss Lawson.* He smiled to himself, lit a cigarette and afterwards threw out the butt onto the wide open Montana landscape.

Chapter 3

After a night of fitful sleep and dreaming of Tom and their last dinner, Teri woke up early and decided to take a drive into town to buy some groceries and supplies for her stay. How long she was staying she was not sure. But the thought that her Uncle was nearby, even in spirit, was a comfort to her. As she drove into the small town, really a village, she marveled at how small and completely alien life there looked compared to New York. However, she marveled at the land's natural beauty and desolateness. Only one highway surrounded by ponderosa pine trees went through the town, and Terri noted a small supermarket, what looked to be a general store called Dollar Town, a handful of offices, a car wash, and then the Clearview Café Jake had mentioned to her.

The café was a pretty nondescript stucco box type building. A flashing neon sign read "Clearview C fe" with the light for the "a" obviously burned out. Despite the early hour, the parking lot already looked full.

"Wow, must be nice to have no competition," Terri said to herself as she pulled into the one empty parking space. She decided she would see if she could meet this Sally that Uncle Bud had been dating and get a spot of breakfast before buying her supplies. In the afternoon, she only planned on taking a nap, exploring the grounds of the ranch more, reading a new romance novel from her favorite writer, Madison Martin, and enjoying the peace and quiet of country life. Her goal was to try and forget New York and take care of herself physically, emotionally and spiritually. A lofty goal, but she was determined to give it her all.

As she walked into the diner, Clearview Café, she found all eyes on her and a hush among the crowd. All the stares began to make her a little uneasy. Obviously, this was not a place used to seeing a new face.

"Well, hon, have a seat. You visiting Clearview?" a voice asked.

Terri turned around to find a woman who appeared to be in her fifties with a large blonde 60's style beehive hairstyle and bright red lipstick. She wore a welcoming smile on her face and smacked a wad of gum in her mouth. She almost looked like a sitcom cliché, but there was warmth to the woman that made her instantly likeable. Her bright smile and twinkle in her eyes radiated a friendly charm.

"My name's Sally. I'm the proprietress of this here fine eating establishment and I'll be helping you today. The pancakes are good enough to make you slap your grandma down, but the waffles are only so-so."

Sally motioned Terri to a seat at the counter and handed her a greasy menu. By this time the noise level in the café normalized and the staring had stopped.

"Thank you," Terri said, taking the menu.

Sally studied her for a moment, and then

a look of recognition showed on her face.

"You're Terri, Bud's niece, aren't you?" she said in wonderment.

"I am," Terri said.

"Well, I'll be," she said, holding out dainty hand for shaking. "It sure is good to meet you after all this time. Your uncle sure did love you. We were…uh…good friends."

"I heard," Terri replied with a friendly little wink thrown in.

Sally chuckled and said, "Small towns, I swear."

"I can see what the fuss was all about," Terri said genuinely. Sally had the type of bubbly personality that would have perfectly complimented her Uncle Bud, a man who never met a stranger.

"Why thank you, honey! I must say, I saw some pictures of you, but you're even prettier in person," Sally said beaming.

"Sally, can we get some more coffee over her?" an older man in overalls called out to her.

"Don, can't you see I'm welcoming this new gal in town?" Sally scolded. "You ain't got anywhere to hurry off to. Mindy will be back from her break in a sec."

Terri marveled at her sass, but the older man just laughed and went back to talking to the other men at his table.

"Oh, Bud was a sweetheart! I sure miss him," Sally continued, as if she had not work to be done. "He volunteered for the Historical Society and helped raise funds for the elementary school, too. He always did what he could to help make Clearview a better place."

"I knew there must have been a woman in his life when I saw all those beautiful daisies and poppies planted outside. Uncle Bud never had a green thumb," Terri said, while Sally took it upon herself to pour Terri a cup of coffee.

"I told Bud that place needed a little color, so I took it upon myself. Bud and I…" Sally stopped, and Terri could tell that she was starting to get a little choked up. "We were both two very independent people, and that's why I think we worked so well. We had our separate lives, but we spent some good times together."

"I'm glad he had you then," Terri said, noticing a younger woman in a pink uniform identical to Sally's come out from the back with a coffee pot and refilling cups on various patrons. "I'm just so sorry we are just now meeting. The past year I was so busy I didn't take the time…"

Now, Terri felt her own self getting emotional, and Sally placed a hand over hers.

"Don't you worry, hon. Your uncle knew just how much he meant to you. He was so proud of you. He told me all about his big lawyer niece in the New York City," Sally said.

Terri smiled. She hadn't planned on getting to know anyone all that well while in town. After all, how open would the residents be about a transgendered visitor? She had planned to just stay to herself until she figured out her next steps.

"If you need anything at all while you're in town, you don't hesitate to let me know, honey. I figured you might need some time to decide what to do with the ranch. Bud told me a long time ago he was goin' to leave it to you."

"It's all a lot to think about, but I needed to get out of New York for a few days anyway."

"Everything gone all right since you been here?" Sally said, bringing out some cream and sugar from under the counter. "Hope your stay in Montana has been nice so far..."

"Oh, it's been great, except for the ticket I almost got," Terry said. "Luckily, the officer let me off, and he was quite handsome."

Truth was she had thought about Jake constantly since he escorted her to the ranch. His gallantry caught her as very "un- New York." What a nice change of pace it had been to meet such a gentleman in modern society.

"Oh, Jake, I bet. We've got a small sherrif's force here. Even the sheriff does the regular patrols. No office work around here. Jake," Sally said, practically licking her lips. "Now, that is one tall, cool drink of water. He makes every female heart flutter just by walking into a room. He hasn't met the right woman yet since the..." Sally said pausing, before adding, "You single, sugar?" She pointed at Terri's empty ring finger.

"Um, yeah...I kinda just got out of a relationship," Terry confessed. She hoped Sally wouldn't ask for more details.

"Well, girl, you've got to get back on that

horse and ride again!" Sally said, before lowering her voice. "So to speak."

"One day. Maybe," Terri said quietly.

At that moment, Jake walked in and greeted the customers in the café. His commanding presence caught the attention of every person in the room. Terri couldn't help but think that he looked even more handsome, if that were possible, this morning. She noticed how his uniform contoured the muscles in his arm just perfectly. Such a man would have a pick of any woman he wanted, and in such a small town, he must be even a bigger catch.

He caught Terri's eye, smiled, and walked over. He took off his hat and revealed a thick head of dark brown hair.

"Morning, Sheriff," Sally said. "Just one empty seat left, and it's next to Clearview's beautiful new visitor. Ain't you lucky?"

Jake smiled sheepishly and looked a little shy.

"Coffee, bacon, and eggs. Thanks, Sally."

"Sure thing, darlin'," Sally said, before turning to Terri. "And you, honey?"

"I'll take the same," Terri said, suddenly feeling a little self-conscious around Jake. She thanked God she had taken the time to smooth her curls, put on a little make-up, and a new pink sundress. She eyed him crossing the room as she sipped her coffee from her mug and now this hunk of man was sitting next to her.

"Hello Miss Lawson, I mean, Terri. I just

wanted to say hello. I noticed your car outside and just wanted ask how things were going at the old house," Jake said sincerely.

His dark brown eyes and tan skin were beautiful up close. His skin a bit weathered by the elements and yet looked soft and smooth.

"Thanks again for the escort. I don't think I would have made it through all these little country roads without you," Terri said. "Things are fine up in the house. Except I had an odd visitor yesterday after you left."

Jake sighed loudly and said, "I'm afraid I have an idea."

"You know?" Terri said, surprised.

"My cousin, Carl, huh?"

"Exactly. Your cousin seems intent on my selling the ranch before I've even had time to take a look at it..."

"I'm sorry about that. Carl and I may be related by blood, but it's been my experience that my cousin always misses a good chance to shut up."

"So I shouldn't listen to him?"

"Let's just say he and I have very different ideas on what would be...," he said choosing his words carefully, "...best for Clearview. He works for a company that wants to develop a condo and resort complex here. I think it'll change our town and not for the best. Most folks here like our laidback quiet way of life. You have to make your own decisions, of course. Just don't let my cousin talk you into anything you're not ready for yet."

"Okay, good advice. But there is one other thing you could help me out with at the house…"

"Yes..?" Jake looked at her pretty face intently, feeling protective of the newest resident of Clearview. He had thought of her nonstop since he met her the night before. In addition to her beauty, which included the type of body curves that would make any red-blooded American man take notice, she exuded a type of confidence he always found attractive in women, but he could sense there was a hurt there, too. A vulnerability he felt instinctive to protect. After all his years on the force, Jake's gut feelings had gotten pretty good at telling if someone was running from something whether it be emotional or physical. Terri Lawson struck him as the big city woman trying to get away from something and that intrigued him.

"Know of any good plumbers? There is no hot water in the place! I realize folks might like roughing it, but this city gal needs some hot water," Terri smiled.

"You know, there was always a trick your Uncle did with the water heater when I was working there. I'll stop by early this evening after my shift and show you if you want."

"Oh, that'd be great," Terri said, feeling suddenly flush at the thought of the sheriff paying her a visit after dark.

In the back of the kitchen, Sally peered

from behind the counter at Jake and Terri talking.

"What in the world are you staring at, Sally?" Mindy asked, walking up to get a look herself.

"Ain't nothing like ridin' a fine horse in new country," Sally said smiling.

"Good Lord. Meaning what?"

"Girl, look at those two. You could *feel* the chemistry between them."

Mindy groaned. "Sally, you and I both know that every single gal in the county practically had tried to catch Sheriff Collin's attention, and we both know why no one has."

Sally frowned and said, "He's a young man though. Time will heal his wounds. He can't spend the rest of his life dwelling in the past."

"But that's just the kind of guy he is. Faithful. Dedicated. Maybe to a fault," Mindy remarked, her eyes gazing at Jake. She'd been one of many to have a crush on the charming sheriff.

"We'll see. I hope it changes for him. None of us will ever forget that night, but…"

"But what?" Mindy asked, ignoring poor Don who waved from the dining room for more coffee.

"None of us can afford to live in the past, it just ends up costing the future," Sally said with the wisdom of her years.

Mindy nodded in agreement before heading out to the dining room with the coffee.

Chapter 4

When she arrived back at the ranch house, Terri toddled towards the door trying to balance the two bags of groceries she picked up at the local Grocery 'N Things market. The pickings were slim. No vegan items. No organic fruits. But Terri always considered here self adaptable and found a few things to eat. Coming from New York, she was amazed at the warmth and genuine interest everyone seemed to have in her. As soon as she mentioned she was Bud's niece to the cashier at the supermarket, the tiny older lady threw in a free coconut cake. So far this small town was starting to grow on her.

Fumbling for the keys in her pocket, she noticed a business card sticking out in the crevice of the door. She sat down the bags and pulled the card out. There in glossy print was a picture of the man from yesterday and the name and title, Carl Collins, Agent, Clearview Estates Resort.

"Damn, this guy doesn't give up," Terri said, shaking her head. Hadn't she *just* spoken to him? Why was he being so pushy?

Jake walked into the office of the Clearview Estates Resort to find his cousin sitting at his desk with his legs propped up on it. In one hand, he held the phone and with the other a huge mug of steaming coffee.

"We'll get those signatures by tomorrow, Mr. Johnson. I guarantee."

Jake walked towards the desk and caught his cousin's eye, and Carl nodded to him.

"Sounds great, Mr. Johnson. I'll call you just as soon as I get the fax. And tell the missus 'hello' for me. Talk soon," Carl said, hanging up the phone, sitting upright at his desk, and eyeing his cousin suspiciously.

"Well, hey there, cuz. For what do I owe this visit? You taking a break from serving and protecting the citizens of Clearview County?" Carl said, the sarcasm dripping off of every word.

Without invitation, Jake sat in the chair across from Carl, took off his hat, and sat it on the desk.

"I needed to have a word with you, Carl," Jake said sternly.

"Well, well, fire away, cuz," Carl said, sipping his ever present mug of coffee.

Jake took a deep breath and debated in his head the best way to approach his cousin. The two had been born within weeks of and grew up next to each other. The competition between the two seemed to be on from the word go. Even though they weren't siblings, rivalry always seemed to be the basis of their relationship.

Although, Jake always thought this competition was all in Carl's head. As kids, he could have cared less who got the better grades, who got what position on the football team, who dated what girl. But Carl always seemed obsessed with keeping a scorecard, and Jake had never understood why. He tried to befriend his cousin on a few occasions, but Carl's sense of competition always soured any efforts. Eventually, Jake gave up and decided he and his cousin would never find common ground. It saddened him because he never had a brother, and he thought about how great things could have been between them if only Carl would let bygones be bygones.

"I want you to leave Terri Lawson alone," Jake stated matter-of-factly.

"I don't understand what you mean," Carl said. "Terri who?"

"Drop the act, Carl. I don't have time today. Sell your brand of crazy somewhere else. Leave Bud's niece alone. She just got in town and is trying to deal with her uncle's death. You showing up on the first day ready to close a deal isn't exactly understanding of the woman's situation."

Carl raised an eyebrow obviously surprised that his cousin knew all these details.

"And how exactly did you get a better understanding of the woman's situation? Well, now Jake, I was just stopping by to offer the little lady an opportunity of a lifetime. Clearview Estates is prepared to offer her a mighty nice sum for the plum piece of property. She'd be foolish not to at least *seriously* think about it."

Jake chuckled and crossed his legs, "Just like the great deal you wanted to offer Bud, huh? You knew how *he* felt about your plan to turn Clearview into some mini-resort. I wouldn't be surprised if it was all your harassment about selling the place that led him to an early grave..."

Carl sat his mug on his desk with a loud *thump* and stood up and began to pace around the room.

"Goddamnit, Jake! I will not stand for these personal attacks. I can't for the life of me understand why you're so dead set against us bringing jobs and progress to Clearwater. The opportunities for everyone here would be astronomical. We could give the young people here a real future. Everyone's land prices could go through the roof. As it is, people want to leave town right after high school rather than stick around."

"Some of us want to keep Clearwater the nice peaceful little town is it, Carl. We're doing okay without some big resort development."

Carl stopped pacing, shook his head, and said, "Wake up Jake and join us here in the 21st century. People need progress and jobs."

"Look," Jake said, standing up. "We're never going to agree on this obviously. I want Clearwater to succeed as much as you. I'm a stakeholder, too, but there must be some way besides carving up all this natural beauty and losing all its charms. I'm not sure what the answer is, but all I'm telling you is to back off of

Terri Lawson. Give her some space."

Carl cocked his eyebrow again and said, "Why do you care so much about this little gal who just got into town? You sweet on her? Or are you trying to get the pretty lady to give you the property herself?"

"You never change, do you, Carl? Just *back off*," Jake asserted. "Or you're going to have me to deal with."

Jake grabbed his hat and marched out of the office. He knew that Carl would not let up easily, but he would protect Terri from him if he had to. He owed it to Bud who gave him a job back when he was a young man and needed it to save for college tuition. And, if he admitted it to himself, part of him felt intrigued to find out more about this woman. Bud, who had no children of his own, had never mentioned a niece when Jake worked for him, only a nephew. Such a strange omission. He would've thought about it more but a call to help out a motorist beckoned him to duty.

Despite herself, like a giddy teenager, Terri cleaned up the ranch and put on a fresh white sleeveless blouse and fitted jeans in anticipation of Jake's arrival. She knew she was being silly. There was *no way* she would start anything romantic with anyone in this town. Hell, she wouldn't be ready if she were still in New York, not after the devastation of what Tom did to her. Yet, here she was, a stranger to this small town, staying in her deceased Uncle's home and yet she was concerned with her appearance. Not for herself, but for a tall, dark stranger who also happened to be sheriff. Interesting how life throws things at you when you least expect. She understood why Sally described Jake as the best catch in town. Hell, he probably was the best one in the whole county. So why wasn't he snatched up? Terri had a hunch there was a story in there somewhere. And if luck was on her side, she might just find out a little more about Sheriff Jake Collins.

When she heard a knock on her door around seven, her stomach practically flipped in anticipation. If she had been excited before, it doubled when she opened the door. For the first time, she saw Jake out of his uniform in a red flannel shirt with the cuff rolled up and a pair of dark blue Wranglers. He looked like one of the dreamy cowboys on the cover of a romance novel. *This is too good to be true*, Terri thought to herself. But, here he was and standing right before her in all his handsome ruggedness.

"Oh, hi. Thanks for stopping by."

"I wanted to stop by earlier, but I had to run home and shower and change. I helped a woman change a tire in a gigantic mud puddle. I was a big mess! I had mud all over me," he confessed.

Terri thought she sort of liked the idea of seeing him all dirty and muddy just as much as she enjoyed seeing him fresh and clean.

"No problem. Come on in," Terri said,

opening the door and motioning for him to enter.

"Thanks," he said, pausing a second before walking inside. Their eyes locked for a moment, and both of them couldn't help but smile.

"It's sweet of you to stop by. Cold showers are not any fun," Terri said smiled.

The more Jake looked at her luscious curls, her delicate neck, and tiny waist the more he thought he might need one of those cold showers when he got home. He hadn't felt this way about a woman in a long time. His tough exterior was rapidly breaking down in front of this captivating woman.

"Let's hope I remember the water heater trick," he said. "Why don't we head out there and see?"

The two went outside and began to walk to the back of the house where the water heater was located. Jake nervously tried to think up some small talk. Usually, he never found himself at a loss for words, but this woman left him tongue tied.

"So, how long you planning on being here?" he asked finally.

"I'm not sure yet. It depends. I'm a lawyer in New York and on a short leave of absence. But I'm sure they won't let me stay too long."

"A lawyer, huh? Smart woman. I'm impressed."

"Well, thanks. It's long hours, but sometimes it's rewarding if I'm working on a case I really believe in."

"That's too bad about your not staying too long. There's a lot to see and learn about Montana if you take the time—and with the right guide."

"Oh, really? I guess I'm not used to taking time. Things just move too fast in New York."

"Clearview must be a real change for you then," Jake said, walking up to the rusty water heater and fiddling with some knobs in the back while Terri looked on.

"True enough!" Terri exclaimed. "It's nice though. People are so much nicer here. And I like the more relaxed pace. I needed a change and a break from my work."

"Don't your husband and kids miss you back in the city?" he asked, glancing back at her. He tried not to sound *too* obvious as he fished for information.

She awkwardly looked away, and immediately Jake thought he put his foot in his mouth.

"Uh..." Terri stuttered.

"I'm so sorry. None of my business," Jake said. "Small town habit. We tend to ask too many questions."

"No, it's okay. I don't mind. Obviously, my uncle thought a lot of you. And to answer your question, I don't have a husband or kids back in New York. You? Have a family, I mean?"

Jake shook his head and answered

quietly. "Nope. Single here."

Terri flashed him a surprised look. "I find that hard to believe."

Jake chuckled and asked, "Why's that?"

"A handsome man in uniform like you would attract women like bees to honey," she replied, immediately wishing she hadn't said that. She had no business flirting or giving out the wrong signals.

Even with his tan complexion, Terri could see him blush.

"Well, thanks. Always nice to get a compliment...from a beautiful lady."

They stood there in silence for a beat before Jake said, "Well, I did some twiddling with the knobs. The pilot light looks like its working. Why don't we wait a few minutes and then check the water temperature?"

"Sounds good," Terri said, wondering what they would do in the meantime. Whit the slim pickings at the grocery store, she didn't have time to get her stock her usual wine and hors d'oeuvres. "Oh, my. Where are my manners? Would you like something to eat or drink? It's the least I can do for you coming all the way out here."

"I had a bite, but something to drink would be nice."

"I'll get that for you."

"You see the lake yet?"

"Lake?"

"Yeah, your Uncle has a lake just a little past those trees out there," he said, pointing out towards a field of trees.

"I had no idea," Terri said in wonderment. She never imagined she would have her own lake.

"Why don't you get yourself something to drink, too, and we'll walk out there and show you? I told you there's a lot to Montana if you take time to explore it."

"I may have to make time," Terri replied.

"Oh, my God!" Terri said, holding a glass of freshly made lemonade and staring out at the body of clear water before her as the setting sun cast crimson, pink and orange streaks across the cloudy sky. "It's absolutely gorgeous."

"Yeah, it really is," Jake said.

He found himself impulsively placing his hand on the small of her back and kept it there while saying, "He built a little pier out this way. Come on, and I'll show you."

They continued to walk along the edge of the lake, the only sounds being of birds chirping in the background as the day began to draw to a close. Terri felt very comfortable with this new acquaintance. She thought he had a nice firm but warm touch. Finally, they reached a small wooden pier that extended about twenty feet out into the water, and Jake led her to the end of it.

"It's so peaceful out here," Terri said in amazement. The loud noises of traffic and people in New York might as well have been on another planet. She began to understand more and more what had drawn her uncle here. There was a quietness that was very calming to the soul and the air was crisp and fresh. Terri felt her senses were being awakened by the natural beauty of it all. So different from the loud and brash city.

"When we were younger, Bud used to let me and Carl come out here on the days we weren't arguing too much and let us fish. That's why he wants the land you know," Jake said, leaning on the railing and watching a school of tiny fish below.

"Because of fishing memories?"

"Because this lake, which is called Lake Crow, would be an excellent spot for his company to build their condos and lakeside resort. The man who owned this land before your uncle, Victor Johansen, had no family, and he and Bud became friends. After he died, he left the land that included the lake to your uncle. Originally, Bud only owned a few acres around the ranch. It ate Carl up inside that he couldn't work out a land deal with Old Man Johansen the first time around."

"I had no idea. I wish...I wish..."

"Wish what?"

"That I would have taken the time to come out here and visit. While Uncle Bud was still alive."

"Why didn't you?"

A cool breeze began to come off the lake, and it blew Terri's soft curls around her face.

"I was always busy. Law school. Then career. And Uncle Bud always made it a point to come out to New York to watch a few shows on Broadway and see me a couple of times a year," Terri said, mournfully. She leaned against the same railing as Jake and their bodies were as close as two can be without touching.

"I regret it now," she admitted. "Especially now that I'm here."

"Well, no better time than the present. Now that you are here, he must have thought a whole lot of you to leave you this place. Him leaving you the place he loved so much tells me a lot about you."

"Thank you, Jake. That means a lot to me," Terri said.

"Do you have a brother?" Jake asked.

Taken aback, Terri moved away from Jake a few inches. "Why?" she asked, sounding defensive.

"Uh, it's just..." Jake started to say. Her reaction to what he thought to be such a simple question perplexed him. Was there some sort of bad blood in the family? "I remember way back Bud used to talk a lot about a nephew he had that lived in the city. I just assumed..."

"Well, uh..." Terri was struggling to come up with an answer when a loud crack and pop came from the railing which suddenly began to give way. Her head was pitching forward into the water and Terri could see her reflection in the still water. But for a brief moment—a mere blink—it wasn't her face she saw but that of her old self, Terrence. She blinked again and he was gone.

Jake immediately reached out, grabbed her, and pulled her back, holding her tightly next to him.

"Whoa! Careful! I should have warned you that this pier was built quite a while ago. I think some of the wood needs to be replaced," Jake said, still holding on to her. He noticed that she made no effort to pull away.

Startled, Terri tried to catch her breath. "Thanks! I was almost swimming with the fishes down there."

"You okay?" Jake said, noticing she still appeared shaken.

"Definitely. Thanks to you," she answered. She felt herself become flush at the thought of how her body felt pressed against his hard one. It was getting colder and she wanted to feel enveloped in his strong arms and pressed against his warm body. Even though she hated to admit it, she missed having a man hold her, making her feel safe and loved.

"Whatever happened to..." Jake started to say.

Terri sensed he was returning to the subject of Bud's nephew and desperate to avoid the brother topic she said, "Would you mind if we go check that water temperature now? I really could use a nice, hot shower after that long drive yesterday."

There was no reason to reveal more about herself to anyone here, the sting of Tom's rejection still fresh. She would only be here for a few days at most just long enough to decide what to do with the ranch. That's what she decided in New York and that was the plan she was going to stick to. This handsome stranger would not deter her from her goal.

"Sure," Jake answered, her avoidance of the brother question didn't escape his sheriff sensibilities, but he decided it was better not to push the topic. If there was something she wanted him to know, she'd tell him. Although, Jake couldn't help but wonder why Bud didn't leave at least part of the ranch to the nephew he spoke of so fondly.

After they checked the water in the kitchen and hot water finally began to flow, Terri thanked Jake profusely. "Thank you so much! You're a genius!"

"Hardly," Jake responded. "I just happened to be here a few times when Bud had to fix it."

Jake took a deep breath and tried to ignore the urge he had to take this woman in his arms and kiss her. The whole evening he'd thought about how good her lips would taste and how her soft, delicate neck would feel against his cheek. Sure, he had had his share of women in Clearview make a play for him, but no woman had managed to catch his eye this way in a very long time. He wasn't a saint, but he wasn't a player either. He respected women and felt it was his duty to honor the badge he wore.

"I should probably let you get some rest," he said, fighting the urge to make a move. He should be a gentleman. This was Bud's niece after all. All woman deserved respect, but he felt a particularly strong need to look out for Terri because she was Bud's family.

She walked him to his truck. The evening had grown quite cool, and the moon shone brightly in the barely cloudy sky.

Jake thought she looked stunning in the luminous moonlight, and she smelled so sweet, like the sweetest spring flower. He held out his hand to be shaken, and he felt her soft yet strong hand in his.

"I really appreciate this and all you've done for me, Jake. You've made me feel very welcomed in town. I don't know what I would've done without you," she said.

"Anything you need. You let me know," he said.

They stood like that for a moment, and she impulsively thought of approaching him for a hug when she noticed two glowing eyes staring at her by the trees, and a fear rushed into her.

"What is that?" she said, jumping back.

Jake turned around to see instantly what he recognized as a coyote.

"Just one of them coyotes coming out. Don't worry. They're just as scared of you as you are of them. They're just curious. Just don't get to close and you'll be fine."

"I'll take your word for it," Terri said, not

entirely convinced. Country living would definitely take some getting used to.

"Hope to see you again," he said, trying to shyly express his interest.

"Me, too," she said, reaching out and placing a hand on his arm before she even realized it.

Terri watched the taillights from Jake's car grow dimmer in the distance. She sighed deeply while the crickets started their peaceful evening symphony and a slight wind blew through the trees.

Why couldn't she find a man like that? Strong and caring, not to mention movie star handsome. Did any men like him even exist in New York City? And if by a miracle she found a man like that, would he love her for exactly the person she was? Or did romance, as she had begun to suspect, only exist in Hollywood movies? She went back into the house and shut the door, eager for a hot shower and warm bed so that she could process the day's events.

Off in the distance, beyond where the coyote had stood, a pair of binoculars was fixated on the Terri and Jake's farewell. The lone figure sat the binoculars on the passenger seat of his Yukon and grunted as Terri entered the house.

"Cuz does have the hots for the new lady in town," Carl said to himself, before taking the final drag on a nearly burned out Marlboro.

"There's no way in hell I'm going to let some bitch from the city ruin this deal when I'm finally so close. No matter *what* I have to do, I'm gonna seal the deal so help me."

His cellphone rang, and he reached into the front pocket of his worn Wranglers to pull it out.

"Talk to me," he answered.

He paused to listen to the caller for a moment before saying, "The minute you have something on her you get back to me. There's got to be something. Everybody has *something.*"

And if he could somehow stick it to his upstanding member of the community cousin at the same time by digging up some dirt on his new lady friend, all the better. After all, Jake deserved it. Sherilynn was supposed to be his. She was so beautiful and sweet and funny. Carl had his eye on her ever since they were in grade school and Jake knew it. Before Carl even had a chance to ask her out in high school, Jake came along to spoil everything. Jake always spoils everything. Sherilynn *could have* been his if he had the chance. But Jake stole her. It was Jake's fault Carl didn't have her. And it was Jake's fault that Sherilynn *died*. It was time for Jake to pay.

This time, Jake, I'm coming out on top, Carl thought to himself.

Chapter 5

Right before lunch the next day, Jake pulled into the near empty parking lot of the Clearview Café. He looked up at the sky and noticed that it had turned a dark, almost black, blue. The wind had started to whip up and leaves blew through the air. *Storm's coming,* he thought instinctively.

He got out of the squad car and could feel the cool crisp air as he walked into the diner to find Mindy reading a fashion magazine and Sally watching the news on a small thirteen inch TV she kept on the counter.

"The usual, hon?" Sally asked him as he sat the counter of the Clearview Café while handing him a menu.

"Sure," Jake answered.

"Mindy, hon, go start Jake's BLT and fries," Sally said.

Looking a little annoyed, Mindy grunted, sat down her magazine, and walked back into the kitchen.

"I don't think I've ever seen this place so empty," Jake commented.

"It's this weather. Those clouds look downright scary. I'd be home too if I didn't own this place," Sally replied. She paused for a moment, and then said, "So, you going to the MontanaFair?"

Jake knew Sally well enough that her tone suggested she was getting at something. He knew Sally too long to not be able to read between the lines.

"Oh, I don't know. Maybe," he said evasively.

She poured him a Coke out of the fountain and sat it in front of him.

"'Cause I was thinking."

"I'm scared to ask," Jake said, raising an eyebrow.

She playfully reached out and slapped him on the arm.

"Oh, come on now," she said, trying to sound all innocent. "I was just thinking maybe you should ask Bud's niece to go with you."

Jake moaned and said, "Sally, are you trying to play matchmaker *again*?"

Sally leaned across the counter and placed a hand over Jake's.

"Darlin', I know it's hard for you to go out with someone, but it's been a long time since…"

Jake shook his head and said, "Look, Sally. I appreciate what you're trying to do, but…"

"But nothing! I saw the sparks between you two yesterday. Don't you even try to deny it! What's it going to hurt taking a nice beautiful woman to the fair for an evening and show her some of the finer points of our state? Who better to do the job than the town's most eligible bachelor sheriff?"

Jake chuckled, "You're impossible."

"You know I'm right," Sally replied,

putting a hand on her hip. "I'm not asking you to marry her. Just go out and have a good time. Sometimes I worry about you. You're too fine to waste! You think about think about that while I go check on your BLT."

She walked back into the kitchen just as Mindy slid the sandwich off a spatula onto a plate.

"Sally, you're really something," Mindy said, shaking her head.

"What do you mean?" Sally responded, shrugging her shoulders.

"Trying to get Jake to ask that woman out," Mindy said, setting a piece of parsley on the plate. "Every available woman in this county, including yours truly, has made a point of flirting with the sheriff, but he's still committed to…"

"I know, I know," Sally said, waving her hands. "But how long can he put his life on hold? *She* wouldn't want that. She would've wanted to see him happy."

Mindy sadly nodded in agreement, and Sally grabbed the plate and headed back out into the dining room.

"Can I get that to go?" Jake said, standing up.

"Now, hon, don't be mad at me."

"No, it's not that. You know I love you. You're practically family. I just got a call from the station. A tornado was spotted about five miles from here in Twin Roses."

"Oh, dear Lord," Sally said, glancing out

the window to take another look out the window. The clouds had grown even darker and hard drops of rain began to pellet the diner's glass windows. "Be careful, Jake."

She handed him his lunch in a take-out container.

"I will. Going to head back to the station in case I'm needed there. You and Mindy keep an eye out, and don't hesitate to run away from the windows at the least bit of a sign of trouble."

Terri had slept in until a very late for her ten thirty. She never slept late back in New York and even got up at six o'clock on the weekends to go running. It felt luxurious to not have a schedule for once.

After sitting on the back porch sipping her coffee and having a blueberry muffin, she headed back inside to start the task of familiarizing herself with what her uncle left behind. It felt beyond strange going through someone else's things and also knowing that she would have to be the one to decide what to do with all of it. She was well versed in legal work, but not being an executor of her uncle's estate. She didn't realize how emotional it would make her feel.

She wasn't aware of how much stuff Uncle Bud had until she ventured into his closets. His clothes smelled of his cologne and she could feel his presence in the massive bedroom with the gorgeous picture window.

On the top shelf in his bedroom closet,

she found an old shoebox of photos, and inside she found one of her as Terrence, the boy. Her parents and Uncle Bud were also in the picture. She suddenly found herself flooded with memories and more regret that she didn't spend more time with her uncle these past few years. It had been so easy to get wrapped up in the little details of life like work obligations and to neglect the truly big parts like family.

The house phone rang startling her. It was the first time the phone in the house while on her visit. She didn't know who it could be, and she sure as hell hoped it was not that smarmy cousin of Jake's. She was definitely not in the mood for him.

"Hello?"

"Hey, it's Sally! Girl, how ya doin' in that big old house?" she asked in her ebullient way.

"Oh, I've been going through Uncle Bud's things this morning...," she said.

"Oh, darling, I'm sorry. I know that's got to be tough. It's hard for me to think about...him not being out there anymore."

"I know you have to be mourning, too."

Sally stayed quiet on the other end for a moment before finally saying, "I just try and remember the good times, you know? He would've wanted that. Your Uncle Bud loved life."

Terri picked up the picture of when they were on Coney Island. She'd always felt unbelievably awkward and out of place as a child. Only when Uncle Bud was around with his fun-loving attitude did she momentarily forget her pain.

"I know. I'm trying to do the same thing, too, Sally."

"I don't know if you'd had a chance to look outside lately…"

"Looks like a major storm is on the way," Terri said looking out the picture window at the ominous clouds gathering over the Montana landscape.

"Well, they spotted a tornado a few miles from town. So, keep your eyes out."

"A tornado!" Terri repeated. Rain began to pelt the ground, and the sky had grown so dark it could almost be mistaken for nighttime outside.

"I wanted to make sure you knew. If you need it, your uncle has a door in the kitchen that leads to the basement."

"Thanks for letting me know. I've been so engrossed in looking through Uncle Bud's things I haven't paid any attention to what's going on outside."

"I know what else I wanted to tell you. The MontanaFair starts tomorrow. Maybe Jake should take you. Show you around. I'll ask him to."

"Oh, I don't know about that," Terri said hurriedly. "I'm so busy right now, and…"

"Exactly! That's why you need to get out of the house for a bit. And well, I gotta tell you I saw the spark between you two yesterday. The way you two looked at each other almost caught my café on fire. I swear!"

"I appreciate what you're trying to do, Sally."

"Hmmm, where else did I hear that today?"

"But, I just recently got out of a relationship."

Sally says, "If you get thrown from a horse…"

"I know I should get back on. But it's just too soon, and I'm only here for a couple of weeks at the most."

"So what's the harm then? Ain't nothing bad about having a good time."

"I just can't…"

And then Terri heard the noise. At first, it sounded like a train far, far away in the distance. The noise grew louder and louder. Then a boom echoed in her ears. She turned towards the window to look out.

"Terri, hon, you still there?" asked Sally.

Terri's jaw dropped when she pulled back the curtains for a look.

"Oh, my God, Sally!" she said, dropping the receiver onto the wooden floor where it landed with a hard crash.

Chapter 6

When Jake heard over the sheriff radio that the tornado had been spotted not far from Bud's old ranch he felt a surge of concern. An instinct told him that he needed to ride out that way to check on Terri to check on her now that the storm eventually dissipated. Jake had seen firsthand the unexpected sudden destructive violence a twister could leash on a community.

As he drove closer to the ranch in the sheriff car his worry grew. The tornado had made a path of ruin along the two lane highway. Trees that had dotted the road for decades were snapped like toothpicks, and the path of obliteration appeared to head straight towards Bud's ranch.

Jake hit the gas, switched on the sirens, and sped towards the ranch. He hoped...he prayed...that Terri was safe.

The small dirt road leading to the ranch was blocked by a fallen pine tree, so Jake stopped the car and hurried out. He jumped over the shattered trunk of the tree and began to run towards the ranch. The home appeared to be intact which eased his mind.

"Terri!" he called out. "Terri, are you okay?"

Being a city gal, Jake didn't know if Terri had the first clue what to do in the event of a tornado. He felt a pang of guilt for not thinking of telling her about the storm cellar on the property. His logical mind told him there had been no way he could have predicted the tornado, but his heart told him he had failed her. Failed her just like...

"I don't think you should go out in this, Sherilynn," Jake said, pulling his fiancée to him and placing kisses on her neck. "Stay here with me tonight and keep me warm. It's cold out there." He couldn't believe how much he cared for this woman and felt truly blessed she was in his life.

She had been the prettiest girl in high school. He remembered when she first arrived in town to help take care of her homebound grandfather. While the other high school students would worry about trivial things like what to wear or which party to go to that weekend, she'd be at home making sure her grandfather's needs were taken care of. She was so selfless. That was one of the things he liked best about her.

"Now Jake, you know if I stay here tonight the last thing we're going to do is sleep. My shift at the clinic starts at five in the morning, and I've got to get some rest," Sherilynn said, giggling and placing one last kiss on his cheek.

She had just started her nursing career at the local clinic, and Sherilynn was determined to make a good impression. Also, now that they were engaged, she wanted to save money for their new life together. She was so ecstatic when Jake proposed. She made a promise in her mind that she would make Jake the happiest man in Montana.

"I suppose I'll let you go," Jake said, running his hands through her ginger curls and giving her another kiss on her pretty pink mouth. He felt an instinct to protect her, even though her fierce independent streak was strong enough for the both of them.

A loud booming sound rocked Jake's tiny cabin, and a flash of violent light shot through the living room window indicating inclement weather approaching.

"Seriously, Sherilynn, I think you should stay here. It sounds like it's getting rough out there. I don't like the idea of you being out there on the road in this."

Sherilynn sighed loudly. She was a strong, stubborn one who had worked her way through college and stood on her own two feet ever since her grandfather passed away. Sometimes her stubbornness drove him nuts though. Once she set her pretty little mind on something, there was no changing it. And usually she was right.

"I'm a big girl. It's just a little rain. I'll be fine. I'll call you when I get home. Love you," she said placing a finger on his lips indicating the discussion was over.

Jake stayed up and waited for the call that never came. The rain had increased steadily and the wind howled, causing the lights in the cabin to flicker. After an hour and no answer on her cellphone, he grew increasingly concerned. Finally, he couldn't take it anymore. He jumped into his car and took off down the highway headed to Sherilynn's grandfather's house. His heart twitched and his stomach twisted the moment his headlights illuminated Sherilynn's car in the pitch dark, now nothing more than an unrecognizable twist of metal which had crashed into a tree. Lightning had struck the tree, and it fell across the highway. She probably never saw it coming in the heavy rain.

His foot hit the brakes, and his car skidded to a stop on the slippery highway. He jumped out of his car and rushed over to the scene, cold rain pouring down his face and soaking his clothes.

"Sherilynn!" he screamed out, praying that somehow she was okay. Somehow she walked away from this. She had to have been okay. She had to. They had their whole future together.

His few years on the sheriff's force had already given him a sixth sense to know when it was too late. When he made it to the car, his eyes landed on her lifeless figure slumped over the steering wheel. Tears poured down his already rain soaked face and he let out a cry of grief as the thunder raged on. The love of his life, his fiancée Sherilynn, was dead. If it had been possible, he would have wished himself dead that very moment, too...

"Terri!" Jake continued to call as he ran towards the ranch, jumping over fallen branches and smaller trees. An eerie sense of déjà vu tingled in the back of his mind which he tried to mentally push away.

"Jake! Thank God!" he finally heard her yell back.

And then she appeared, running out of the ranch and straight towards him. She didn't stop until she instinctively threw herself into his arms. Jake held her tightly, with all of his might, almost hugging the breath out of her, thankful she was alright.

He pulled back and took a good look at her. Her face had turned an almost ashen pale shade, and she appeared to be trying to catch her breath.

"Are you okay?" he asked, gripping her shoulders.

All she could do was nod before throwing herself into his strong arms again.

Jake embraced her as he scanned the area around them.

"My God! It's a miracle!" he exclaimed.

Fallen tress surrounded the entire ranch house, but not one single tree had fallen on the house.

Terri reluctantly left Jake's arms and took in the complete damage for the first time herself.

"I thought I was going to die," she said softly.

The moment she saw the tornado, she

dropped the phone and had run into a bedroom closet to try and shield herself from the windows. The sound of the tornado became deafening, and Terri thought her heart would beat out of her chest. The smell and warmth of Uncle Bud's old clothes surrounded and comforted her. She thought of and tried to focus on his smiling face as the storm raged outside. Loud snapping sounds filled the air. But just as soon as it appeared, the tornado passed over and a peaceful quiet settled in the house once more.

"You're okay," Jake said reassuringly, and without thinking twice about it took her hand into his. "I can't believe it, not one tree hit the house. Someone up there is watching over you, Terri."

"Uncle Bud," Terri said quietly. In her heart, she believed that her uncle had looked out for her from beyond. How else could such a miraculous event occur?

"Come on," Jake said, leading her towards the ranch, "Let's go in and sit for a moment. I know where Bud kept his scotch, and I think you could use a shot right now."

"Yeah, I agree," she replied, following him and holding his hand even tighter. This simple touch between them felt so natural, so easy...in a way she had never even felt with Tom who she thought she loved more than life itself. She was so grateful for having a strong, masculine figure like Jake in her life.

As they neared the house, the sun cut through the clouds and illuminated an uprooted ponderosa tree. A slight glimmer near the roots caught Terri's eye.

"Wait a sec," she said, leading him to the knot of tangled roots.

"What is it?"

"I see something shiny in the roots of that tree."

When they got close enough to inspect it further, Jake muttered, "Well, look a there."

There in between the roots were fragments of what looked to be shards of multi-colored pottery. An array of different pieces with colorful designs seemed to have been preserved under the tree.

"What is it?" Terri asked.

Jake knelt down, picked up one of the clay pieces, and held it up to the light.

"Looks like Native American pottery pieces from one of the tribes that lived in this area. Possibly the Crow people."

Terri bent down to have a closer look herself. "There looks like a lot of it," she said, amazed. "How long do you think it was buried?"

"That's a good question. I don't know. But there is someone who would. An old professor I had in college, Professor Redfeather, is an expert on the local history. I'd like to call him to come take a look at this if you don't mind. He lives nearby and does a lot of work with preserving and cataloging Native artifacts."

"Of course. I've love to learn a little more about these pieces. Maybe it's an important find! It'd be nice if something good comes from all of this," she said, pointing to the all the storm debris.

"I know some good guys who would be happy to help you clean this up, too, if you let them keep the wood," Jake said.

"That'd be great. I wouldn't even know where to start," she said surveying the littered landscape. He practically read her mind. How wonderful.

She noticed Jake looked mesmerized studying one of the pottery pieces.

"I'm part Native American, you know," he said softly.

"Really?" Terri said. That explained his handsome, dark features. His cousin Carl looked more typical all American apple pie.

"Yeah. My maternal grandmother was Crow," he said, remembering the kind old woman who would always weave him a new sweater every Christmas. Carl would often tease him when they were children, calling him "half-breed" in front of the other neighborhood kids. They would make him play "Indian" to their cowboys.

"I hated being part Native growing up. Not only were they bad guys in the western movies, but sometimes I'd see alcoholic Indians begging on the streets of town or committing crimes around the reservation. At the time, I didn't understand what was really behind some of that. When I got older I found himself wishing I had learned more about that part of my culture from my grandmother before she passed.

Her last words to me were, 'You should be proud of your Native heritage. Learn the wisdom of ancestors.'"

He looked at Terri, who was listening intently, fascinated by his sharing of something personal to her.

"Those words led me to take Professor Redfeather's Native American Studies class," he continued. "The bespectled, long dark haired man opened up a new world for me and gave me insight into the past of my Native ancestors. How they were masters of the land and respected nature's natural rhythms and cycles. How in many tribes men and women were equal. And how helping others, such as the English Colonists, was ingrained in their culture. I guess you could say my becoming a sheriff is ingrained in me!"

"Thank you, Jake, for opening up to me. I didn't realize…," Terri said. Terri thought to herself how this man in all of his authority but sensitivity had to be one of the sexiest men she'd ever seen.

"What I found it ironic is that only now is modern society relearning green principles that were respected by Natives for thousands of years. I guess that why I butt heads with my cousin Carl so much…"

Jake's phone rang momentarily interrupting their moment together.

"Collins," he answered.

He hung up the phone and said, "There's been some accidents down the highway I need to go check out, but I don't want to leave you..."

"No, go," Terri said, placing a hand on his chest. She could feel his heart beating through the fabric of his uniform. What she would give to lay her head on his chest at night, his strong arms enveloping her. She could only imagine the sense of serenity that would bring her. "You have a duty, and I'll be fine."

He looked at her, obviously hesitating. It had been years since he felt this drawn to any woman, not since his fiancée...

"Are you sure?" he asked one more time, a bit uncertainly.

"Yes, definitely. You're needed," Terri said, taking a deep breath and putting on a strong face. "I'll take some time assessing the rest of the damage. I okay. Thanks again for being there for me."

"No problem. Be very careful walking around."

"I will."

He started to head back to his patrol car, but abruptly turned back around and said, "I'll stop by and check on you later."

Terri thought it almost sounded like a question, a request for permission.

"Thanks. I would really like that," she replied because she couldn't think of anything more wonderful that moment that seeing this man once again. Even though her brain told her to shield her heart, it was exactly her *heart* that was unmistakenly drawn to Jake.

She wrapped her arms around herself,

wishing they were his strong, sinewy arms, as she watched him hurry back to his car.

In the background, she heard a distant ringing and realized it was her phone. Dodging fallen twigs and branches, she made her way back to the house and picked up her cell phone right before it went to voicemail. It was Martin calling from the office in New York. What a pleasant surprise, she thought.

"Hello?" she answered breathlessly.

"Terri, is that you?"

"Oh, Martin, you have no idea what just happened. Is work okay?"

"Forget about work! I wanted to check on you, and see how your trip is going."

"Well, I just survived my first tornado."

"*Seriously?*"

"Unfortunately, yes. But I'm okay, and amazingly, so is the ranch. A few fallen trees but nothing major."

"Well, I'm glad to hear that. I've been...worried about you."

She was truly moved by Martin's words. She'd been so lost in her fog of hurt and rejection between Uncle Bud dying and Tom leaving her that a friendly voice from back home made a huge difference.

"I'm okay. Life is definitely...*different* here. But it's nice."

"Have you met some people?" Martin asked.

She paused momentarily. "Yes, I have, actually," she said with a little lilt in her voice.

"Ah. You've met someone. There's a story there. C'mon, tell Uncle Marty everything…" Martin said, knowing her too well.

"No, Martin, it's not that," she said dismissingly. "Just some sweet people here. That's all."

"Sweet? Is that all, really?"

"Yes, really."

"Oh, okay. I'm a little disappointed. I thought maybe you met your cowboy. Well, have you decided what you want to do with the property yet?"

Had she met "her" cowboy? Terri gazed outside at the huge mess that now was her lawn.

"I'm not sure what to do with the property yet. First, there's a huge mess outside to get cleaned up. How are things in the office?"

"The usual. Nothing that can't wait. Take as much time off as you need! I think you need this time now for many reasons."

Martin had been the only person at work that she confided in about her breakup with Tom.

"Thank you, Martin. You've been very supportive and patient. I'm so confused about so many things right now. *So many things*."

"Well, you're one of the smartest women I know, Terri. If anybody can figure it out, I know you can. I'll talk to you later," Martin said.

"Okay, bye," Terri said, pressing the "end call" button on her phone.

Could she figure things out? Martin had so much confidence in her. Her trip to Montana was supposed to clear her mind. But her thoughts drifted back to Jake and the feelings he stirred within her. Part of her wished she could push them away, reject those feelings just as Tom had rejected her. But worse than any tornado, she feared the storm brewing in her heart for Sheriff Jake Collins.

Chapter 7

Later that night, after accidents in which, thankfully, no one was hurt were cleared, Jake went home, took a quick shower, and then drove out to Bud's ranch wearing jeans, his favorite boots and his cowboy hat. The sudden occurrence of the tornado today and the accidents on the highway reminded Jake how precious, and sometimes chaotic, life could be. Ever since Sherilynn passed away, he'd kept everyone at bay especially the advances of any women. His constant pangs of guilt for letting her drive that evening prevented him from opening up to anyone. He told himself he just couldn't feel that kind of pain again, the kind that he was convinced had to be worse than dying. Survivor guilt. But ever since pulling Terri over on the highway, he felt a spark inside that had been long dormant. Maybe this was a sign. He decided he knew what he had to do, and maybe Terri would be the perfect woman for it since she wasn't planning on staying in town very long.

He pulled his Jeep up to the driveway, leaving work and the patrol car at home. He stepped over the storm debris and strode to the door. He wanted to appear calm, causal, and confident, but inside he felt anything but. He felt like a high school boy again and asking Sherilynn out for the first time.

Jake knocked on the door a couple of

times, and Terri quickly answered. He thought she looked breathtaking in a light blue sundress, her hair pulled back loosely behind her head showing off her delicate neckline.

"Hey there," he said, leaning against the doorway. He quickly decided that that posture looked a little *too* casual, and he stood back up straight. What was it about this woman that made him a bundle of raw, loose nerves?

"Hey there," she said back. "Thanks for checking on me. I've managed to calm down quite a bit. Would you like to come in?"

God, would he ever! But he didn't trust himself. He feared if he took one foot inside that door he would sweep her up into his arms, carry her off to the bedroom, and make urgent passionate love to her that would allow both of them to forget all their troubles from the day. But, Jake was nothing, if not a gentleman.

"Thank you, but I can't stay. I told Sally I'd stop by the diner and help her move some debris."

"Oh, sure," Terri said. She immediately hoped she didn't sound too disappointed. She noticed that even though he wouldn't come inside he appeared to be hesitating.

"There was something I wanted to ask you though," he said, his voice a little shaky.

"Sure."

"Um...well...this may sound kind of corny to a big city gal like you, but there's the MontanaFair happening not far from here this week. There are all sorts of events and a lot of good fried food. I'm off tomorrow, and wondered if maybe you'd want to check it out," he said, feeling a sense of relief for finally getting the question out.

"That doesn't sound corny at all, Jake. Sounds like a fun way for a lady to lose her figure, but if it means going with a guy like you, I'd be delighted," she answered, showing off her cute smile.

A flood of relief swept through Jake's body and he broke out into a huge grin.

"Great. Would nine in the morning be too early to head out?"

"I'm a morning person. So, make it eight-thirty."

He chuckled and said, "You got it, ma'am."

Jake started to head back to the Jeep with a little spring in his step and even he knew his face was still beaming.

Terri closed the door behind after Jake left, and even though it had turned into night, she felt like she was floating on sunshine. She let out a little gleeful cry. She was going out with Jake!

She headed into the kitchen, took out some ingredients to make a small salad, and then went searching through the kitchen drawers looking for a corkscrew to open a bottle of Merlot. She came upon a small photo album with ragged edges in the back of what appeared to be Uncle Bud's all purpose junk catch-all drawer filled with matchbooks, screwdrivers, old newspaper items, etc.

She felt a rush of sadness. Uncle Bud. Why didn't she take more time to spend with him these last few years? She knew why. *Her career.* Before Tom and after her transition, she had made her career everything. She mistook having a career for having a life.

Terri opened the photo album and saw a snapshot of Uncle Bud and Sally on what appeared to be a mountain top somewhere. She found it curious that he never mentioned her. What else hadn't she known? Even those we know the best can still surprise us, she thought.

She turned the page, and she immediately sucked in a breath. It was a picture of her. Actually, it was a picture of *him* or who people knew to be Terrence. Fifteen years old, arms and legs too long for the body, a pimply face, sitting on a park bench but an actual genuine smile. She then remembered it was taken on a trip to Vermont with Uncle Bud. Despite the awkward growing pains, it was one of the few happy moments from her teenage years.

Terri felt a quick sense of dread. Doubt and fear crept into the back of her mind. What was she doing going out with Jake tomorrow on what was obviously a date to him? They were from two completely different worlds. Should she be upfront with him now? She pondered the thought of having to have *the talk*, explaining her transition from Terrence to Terri. But all she really wanted to be tomorrow was a girl on a date with a nice guy. Hell, she needed it. Why complicate things? What was the harm in a simple date? Her therapist had always told her to enjoy the present. After all, there could never be a future with Jake. Could there?

Jake dragged a large tree branch to the back of the diner while Sally followed him, excitedly yakking the whole time about that day's weather excitement.

"Swear to you, Jake, I thought I was going to have to bend over and kiss my own ass goodbye when I heard it coming from yonder. Mindy dove under the counter, but then the sound drifted off," she said, one hand on her hip and smacking gum in her mouth. "I'm glad to hear Terri was okay. I tried calling her back. I was so worried about that poor girl all out there by herself."

"She's fine and so's the ranch. I just checked on her again, too," Jake replied.

He picked up the huge branch with his husky arms, like it was a piece of paper and tossed it in the dumpster.

"Ya did, did ya?" Sally said, cocking her head.

Jake felt his face redden. He gave away embarrassment way too easily. He knew now the barrage of questions would begin. If Sally sensed a new piece of gossip, she could be like a hound dog with a meaty bone. She wasn't going to let up on that for anything until she was satisfied.

"Just wanted to make sure she was okay," he said. He flipped the top back over the dumpster.

"And…?" Sally said, digging deeper. "What's going on there with you two?"

"We just met!" Jake protested.

"So, what's that got to do with the price of potatoes in Idaho? I can tell when two people have some...tension, and I mean the good kind between them."

Jake relented. She would find out sooner or later once he was spotted at the fair with Terri the next day. World travels fast in a small town. There were no secrets.

"Well, I did ask her to go to MontanaFair with me tomorrow."

"Hot damn!" Sally said, clapping her hands. She then playfully slapped Jake on the back. "It's about time you got your motor running again. You are just a too damn good looking man not to!"

Jake just shook his head, too embarrassed by the compliment to respond. Trying to change the subject, he said, "You know something? Bud never mentioned a niece when I worked for him. Only a nephew."

"Hmmm..." Sally said, thinking about it for a moment. "He only mentioned his niece to me. Never a nephew."

"Just seemed a little odd to me. Maybe he fell out of contact with the nephew," Jake wondered.

"Maybe," Sally said. "I'm just glad to hear you're dating again."

"Let's not start booking the wedding chapel, Sally."

"I can't help it. I worry about you, son. You're a good man, Jake. You would make any woman happy. And she would be lucky to have you. What happened with Sherilynn...it just wasn't your fault, honey. It was an accident."

Jake nodded, but his facial expression betrayed him. He still wasn't convinced that he didn't play a part in what happened to Sherilynn. If only he had been more insistent. If only...He truly loved her, but he knew instinctively he had to start moving on. Life is for the living, as his grandmother always told him. Maybe, just maybe, Terri, the beautiful stranger from the big city, would remind him what life was all about.

Chapter 8

As Jake and Terri headed down the winding Montana highway in his Jeep, Terri, wearing a sleeveless pink blouse and jeans, took a deep breath of the crisp, clear mountain air and let the warm sun kiss her shoulders. She looked over at Jake and thought how handsome he looked in his cowboy belt and tight in all the right places dark blue jeans.

To while away the time during the drive, he asked about her life in the city and her work. She spoke a little of all the corporate litigations she'd been involved in over the years.

"Work for the big guns then?" Jake said. "Impressive."

"Not always. I do some *pro bono* work for a local nonprofit," she said.

"What kind?"

"Human rights organizations. But let's leave work at work and just have fun today, okay?" she said trying to nip discussion of the details of her work in the bud. The time and place was not yet appropriate for *the talk.*

"Roger that," Jake said, looking at her curiously before his eyes went back to the road.

"Thanks."

Terri took another deep breath of air and decided that today she would just focus on having some innocent fun with a dreamy guy.

MontanaFair, Terri came to learn, was a big deal around those parts. The fair is the region's largest event with attendance of nearly a quarter of a million each year. The fairgrounds were spread out just out the outskirts of Billings and included an arena, an expo center and a racetrack.

"This place is huge," Terri marveled, after they finally found a parking space after driving around for twenty minutes. "I'm pleasantly surprised. Who says there isn't anything to do outside of New York?"

"You just wait, city girl. Montana is full of more surprises," Jake said, opening the passenger door for her. "Let's go get our tickets."

After they entered the fairground, the smell of corn dogs and BBQ, corn on the cob, 'Vikings On a Stick', fresh lemonade, and beer gardens. Also, the sounds of hi-speed rides and competitive games filled the air. As they walked through the grounds, occasionally someone would yell out a "Hey, Jake" from the crowd. Jake would wave hello or tip his hat and give the person a big smile. It seemed to Terri that he knew half the people around.

One older gentleman, wearing overalls and a huge grin, greeted Jake and said, "Hi, Jake. Why your lady friend here, she's prettier than a glob of butter melting on a stack of wheat cakes!"

Terri couldn't help but giggle. That was one compliment she had never heard before.

Montana definitely had its regional charms.

"If you haven't figured it out yet, everybody kinda knows everybody around these parts," Jake said. "Being sheriff, I probably know even more people that most."

"It's a little different in New York," Terri commented. She thought back on the mass of strangers she passed every day with no one making eye contact as their paths crossed for brief seconds in the thriving metropolis.

Jake pointed off in the direction of an enormous Ferris wheel in the distance.

"Feel like a ride?" he asked.

"I haven't been on a Ferris wheel in ages," Terri confessed.

"Well, I think you're overdue then," Jake said, taking her by the hand and leading her off in the direction of the ride.

Once on the ride, the wheel stopped when their car was at the top, and they could see the beautiful view of the surrounding area. Terri couldn't remember the last time she saw such large areas of lush green foliage.

"This is beautiful country, Jake" she mused out loud.

"Over there are the Bighorn Mountains," Jake said, pointing in one direction. " And over there are the Pryor Mountains, the Beartooth Mountains, the Crazy Mountains, the Big Snowy Mountains and the Bull Mountains."

"It's incredible. Very peaceful."

"Not as beautiful as you," he said, taking her hand into his once more.

"The feeling's mutual," Terri replied smiling while flicking the hair away from her eyes. She forgot how good the fine art of flirting felt.

He surprised her by making another move and putting his arm around her thin waist. As their Ferris wheel car began its descent, Jake leaned over and boldly placed a kiss on her lips. Terri found his lips warm and sweet. She cradled his rugged face and kissed him in return, deeply and passionately for what seemed like an eternity.

"Time to get off you two lovebirds," the cranky old ride attendant said, interrupting their romantic interlude while a gaggle of pre-teens waiting in line giggled at them.

As they walked though the rest of the fairgrounds and checked out the competitions in Heritage Arts & Crafts and Culinary, they ran into Sally at a booth wearing a Viking helmet with long light blonde braids coming out of the side.

"Hi, you two!" she said with a smile. "Viking on a Stick?" Sally held up a large round fried ball with a stick coming out of it.

"It smells delicious. Umm, what is it?" Terri mused.

"Oh, it's a tradition around here. Just ask Jake. Basically it's a lightly seasoned baked meatball, dipped in a batter and deep fried to a golden brown. Since you're a newbie, here's a free sample! You haven't lived until you've tasted one!"

"What about me?" Jake joked.

"Oh, *pardon mois*, sheriff. Here's one for you. That'll be $2.00 for you though," she winked.

Jake handed over the money to a smiling Sally.

"Who's minding the cafe today?" Terri asked.

"I left Mindy in charge. I always work the fair a few days to help out a local charity. And what do you think so far?" Sally said, cocking an eyebrow.

Terri wondered if she was referring to the fair, the food or the date with Jake.

"So far, I'm impressed," she answered truthfully.

Sally cut her eyes at Jake and grinned devilishly before saying, "I just bet you are."

Terri took a bite of her Viking on a Stick and much to her surprise found herself saying, "Oh my God! This is so good!"

"Well, howdy there!" a booming voice called behind them.

Terri saw Sally practically wince at the sound.

Terri and Jake turned around to find Carl, his wife, Dora, and two boys, Emmet and Dylan.

"Cousin," Jake said, tipping his hat. "How you doing, Dora and boys?"

Terri noticed how haggard and exhausted poor Carl's slightly pudgy wife looked as she tried to wrangle the boys, who looked no older than ten, to stay still for a moment.

"We're doing just fine!" Dora replied. Although, she looked like she was ready to kill both of her children due to some behavior issue.

"This is Terri Lawson, Bud's niece, from New York," Jake said to Dora.

"So, nice to meet you. We were so sorry to hear about Bud."

"Thank you," Terri replied. "That means a lot. Everyone's been so nice and understanding."

"Heard about your little storm the other day. Sounds like you have quite a mess to clean up. Might be the perfect time to sell so you don't have to deal with it," Carl said.

An exasperated Doris elbowed her husband and said, "Carl, can we have one day without business, please? This is supposed to be your day off."

"Just saying. You've got to be ready when opportunity comes along," Carl said, trying to sound all innocent.

"I'm sure I'll figure out how to clean things up," Terri responded. The more this guy pushed her to sell her uncle's ranch, the less she even wanted to entertain the thought. She didn't know for sure what she would do with it, but she didn't want her uncle's legacy in this saleman's hands.

"We best be going," Jake said. He placed a protective hand on Terri's lower back, and she felt her face become flush just from his touch.

The two young boys ran up to Jake and gave him a hug.

"Can we go riding in the patrol car with you again one day, Cousin Jake?" Emmet asked.

"Sure thing," Jake said, patting their heads.

Dylan looked up at Terri and said, "Cousin Jake is the sheriff, you know? He's a hero!"

"That's what I hear," Terri said.

Out of the corner of her eye, she saw a flash of anger sweep across Carl's face.

Carl watched as his cousin and that damn Lawson woman walked off. He got sick of everyone always talking about how much the hero Jake was. Even his own kids were fixated on him. But they would see. Everyone would see. Carl's development projects would be his legacy to Clearview. They would put the town on the map and do more good than anything Jake Collins could ever drum up as sheriff.

"She seems real sweet. Pretty, too," Dora said to her preoccupied husband.

"Hmmm," Carl just grunted.

He felt his cellphone vibrate in his pocket and quickly pulled it out while Dora let out an audible groan.

"I'll be just a few minutes," he said, walking off a few yards when he saw who the caller was.

"Don't be too long, Carl. The boys are ready for lunch and you promised we could go shopping later," Dora called after him.

Carl nodded to his wife as he walked away from the main path to a quiet area behind some booths.

"Talk to me," he said, answering the phone, sure that no one would hear. After listening intently for a couple of minutes, Carl said softly to himself, "You've got to be kidding me! That's good work. Really good. We'll talk later."

After a few minutes Carl ended the call and stuffed his phone into his pocket. He smiled a devilish grin as he walked back to his family.

"Don't look now, but you've got canary feathers all over your face," his wife remarked.

"Who me? No, I'm just *so* glad to see Cousin Jake so happy with his lady friend, Miss Terri. I just hope it all works out for them. Would be a shame if something suddenly came up...," said Carl while his wife looked at him puzzlingly.

Chapter 9

After a full day of enjoying the fair, Jake drove Terri back to the ranch. They kept silent throughout the drive, basking in the dramatic sunset over the dusty road framed by the windshield of the Jeep. The sexual tension between the two was palpable. As the car stopped in the ranch's driveway, the two looked at each other while Jake's motor idled for what seemed like an eternity.

Terri took a deep breath before saying, "I had a really good time today, Jake. It would be a shame to have this perfect day end so soon. Would you like to come in for a drink? I bought a nice bottle of merlot the other day."

She knew what coming in for a glass of wine could mean…second base or more. But she was telling him the honest truth. She'd been having the best day she'd had in such a long time. She didn't want it to end.

"I'd like that. *A lot*," Jake answered.

Jake worked on building a small fire in the living room while Terri nervously uncorked the wine. She poured two glasses, and walked out to the living room to find Jake sitting on the sofa after starting a fire…in more ways than one, she thought!

She sat next to him on the sofa and handed him a glass of wine.

"Cheers," Terri said holding up her glass up to Jake. The glasses tinkled, and she took a little taste of the wine.

After a moment of awkward silence in which they both appeared to be waiting for the other to make the next move, Jake finally said, "I had a really great time today."

"Me, too," Terri replied. "I haven't just enjoyed myself and felt that...relaxed in a long time."

"Sounds like you were due for some time out of the city," Jake said, sipping the wine. He didn't drink much, and when he did, it tended to hit him pretty fast. He could already sense a warm feeling making its way through his body. Terri's closeness stirred deep emotions within him yearning to be expressed. She was so beautiful and smelled so nice. It made him want to pull her close, taste her mouth, and hold her to him until the sun came up in the morning.

"I think you're right. I needed some time away for a few reasons," she paused and took another sip before getting more personal. "I have to admit something."

"What is that?"

"How has a great guy like you managed to be single all these years? I can't believe some nice girl around here hasn't snapped you up yet."

She noticed that he shifted uncomfortably for a moment, and his eyes drifted down to the floor.

"I'm sorry. Did I say something wrong?" she asked anxiously, sitting her wine glass on the coffee table. He suddenly seemed distant and lost in thought.

He took a long deep breath and his eyes met hers.

"Not at all," he said. "I appreciate the compliment. The truth is…I did have a fiancée at one time."

"Oh," she muttered. Her thoughts flooded back to her Tom and the hurt he caused her before she admitted, "I did, too, once."

"Really?" he replied, his curiosity piqued. "What happened? If you don't mind my asking."

"He called it off. A few weeks before I came here," she confessed. "It was one of the other reasons I wanted to come to Montana. To just get away to think things through."

Jake reached over and his strong hand covered hers on the couch.

"Well, it's his loss. You're a great woman."

"Thank you. I appreciate it," she said slightly blushing from the wine and the compliment. "And you? What about your fiancée?"

Jake swallowed hard. It was always so difficult for him to talk about Sherilynn, but he had finally begun to realize that maybe he needed to do so to move on. He felt very comfortable around Terri for some reason. He wanted to open up to her.

"Her name was Sherilynn. We met in high school, and she was my sweetheart. I asked her to marry me, but…it wasn't meant to be. She died in a car accident a few years back."

"Oh, Jake, I'm so sorry!" Terri said, interlacing her fingers around his and squeezing his hand tight.

"I guess..." he started to say.

She could tell he was struggling, and she so badly wanted to crawl into his arms, kiss him, and tell him everything would be okay.

"I guess….I blame myself a lot," he admitted.

"But why? What do you mean," Terri asked confused.

"The weather was very bad the night she died. I tried to talk her out of driving, but when Sherilynn had her mind made up about something there was no changing it. It was something about her that I loved and drove me crazy, but I wonder if I had just tried harder to convince her just maybe..."

"You can't blame yourself, Jake. Accidents happen."

"I know that in my mind, but..."

"In you heart you still wonder," Terri said, finished his thought.

He looked at her with amazement. How did she understand him so well? *So quickly?*

"You're right. I do," he said quietly.

"You're a wonderful man, Jake, and I'm sure your fiancée was an exceptional woman. She'd want you to go on with your life. I know it's easier said than done, though."

"From your own situation?" he asked.

"Yes," she said, nodding.

She took another sip of the merlot and leaned back on the couch.

The whole time they held hands and gazed at each other in a way only two people who feel connected beyond words can.

Until, finally, Jake said, "Come here. I think we both need a hug." He held out his arms for her to cuddle next to him.

Terri couldn't help but beam at the gesture, and she scooted closer next to him. He wrapped his arms around her and pulled her close to him while she buried her face in his hard muscular chest. His masculine scent was so intoxicating she wished she could just melt into him.

With his hand, he lifted her chin and her gaze.

"All day I've been wanting to kiss you again," he confessed. "Ever since the Ferris wheel."

"Really?" she asked, feeling a tingling sensation in the core of her essence she hadn't felt in a very long time.

"May I, Terri?"

"Please," she replied, closing her eyes and puckering her soft, wet lips for this sexy man next to her.

His kiss was at first gentle and sweet, but as he brought her body in closer to his even tighter, he became more passionate, more determined in his expression of physical affection for her.

A voice in Terri's head told her that she should stop him. It was too soon. There was much she needed to tell him first about her and her past. When he leaned her down on the couch though and the weight of his body mixed with the growing hardness of his manhood, she felt herself give in to her desires. She lay there, vulnerable and open, for Jake.

He kissed the delicate skin on her neck, down lower to the top of her bosom, and before going any further he said to her in a husky voice, "I want you so bad. I've wanted you from the moment I saw you." He paused momentarily and said, "But I don't want to rush things if you aren't ready, Terri."

"Oh, Jake, I need you so badly," she managed to half-whisper.

Her heart felt like it would beat straight through her chest as she allowed the weight of him to press her further down into the cushion. She so desperately wanted to take him inside her, to have him complete her in the way only a man like Jake could. It had been so long...

Jake nuzzled his stubble against her neck which almost drove her to the brink of her yearning but conflicted passion. Terri let out a slight cry of pleasure. Before she could say a word, he lifted her off her feet and up the stairs to the bedroom and placed her gently but purposefully on the soft bed.

He began to unbutton his shirt, and when Terri caught a flash of the sight of his hard abs, she couldn't help but quietly, but audibly gasp.

The bright Montana moon shone over the ranch, its light streaming through the bedroom window and illuminating Jake's beautiful body as he began to unbuckle his pants.

Chapter 10

The bright sunlight shone through the bedroom indicating a new day, and Jake noticed how the soft light accented the red highlights in her hair. For the past thirty minutes or so, he had been content with just watching her sleep next to him. She was so beautiful. Being from the city, she seemed so exotic, so different from the other women in town, but they connected so naturally. Jake could picture her as a woman that could challenge him, make him think about things in this world in a different light. His only worry was that he knew she came from this different world and soon it would beckon her to return. And where would that leave him?

He suddenly got the idea of cooking her breakfast so it would be ready when she first got up. It had been so long since he'd been able to do that for anybody. So, he carefully scooted out of the bed so as not to wake her and tiptoed downstairs to see if there were any breakfast items were in the kitchen.

He checked in the fridge and found half a dozen eggs, some link sausage, and coffee. *Good enough*, he thought. He searched through the cupboards to find where Bud kept his pans being mindful not to make too much noise and wake up his sleeping beauty. He hoped they could spend more time together today, and he could show her more of what Montana had to offer.

As he started to fry up the sausage, he heard a light tapping on the front door. Curious as to who would be stopping by at this hour in the morning, he went towards the front door and was stunned to see Carl peeking though the window.

"What the hell?" Jake muttered. The guy just wouldn't give up. He was like a starving dog with a meaty bone. He decided he would make it clear to his stubborn cousin that under no uncertain terms he better back off.

Jake opened the door and shook his head when he saw Carl, already wearing a suit, standing there with an extra large coffee in his hand.

"Well, somebody must have had a good night, cuz!" Carl bellowed with smile.

"That's not really any of your business, is it? Please keep it down. Terri's still asleep," Jake admonished.

Carl raised an eyebrow and replied, "Well, we wouldn't want to wake the *little lady.*"

Jake picked up on more than a hint of sarcasm in his cousin's voice.

"What the hell are you doing here, Carl? Why can't you take a hint? Bud wouldn't sell to you, and obviously Terri is in no rush to make decisions, either."

Carl leaned against the doorway waiting to be invited in, but when he wasn't, he stood back up and said, "I'm worried about you, Jake. I know we've had our differences, but you're still my family. There are things you don't know that you should. When I saw your car wasn't parked outside your place I came rushing over her. I knew I couldn't wait to tell you the truth. You deserve to know the *truth*."

Jake could smell the sausage cooking and realized he needed to get back to breakfast.

"I don't know what the hell you're referring to, and I don't really care. If I see you here one more time, I'll convince Terri to have you arrested for trespassing--family or no family!"

"Well, them's mighty big words, Jake. Especially, when you don't know what a fool that *woman* is making of you. The thing is that woman isn't what she appears to be..."

"Goodbye, Carl. You've stooped to new a new low this time. Don't come back," Jake said, starting to shut the door in Carl's face.

"She used to be a man!" Carl exclaimed, waiting for Jake's expression.

Jake, startled, froze for a second and then chuckled.

"God, Carl! You are something," he responded, before starting to shut the door again.

"I have proof, Jake," Carl said, his stare cold and void of any affection for his cousin.

"You're insane," Jake said but not trying to shut the door this time. There was something in the determined tone of Carl's voice that caught him off guard. The thought was so preposterous even Carl wouldn't be this crazy to try to stir up trouble, would he?

"I hired a private investigator to check her out so I could get a better idea of who she was. Maybe I could get some info to help me negotiate with her. You know, your typical background check."

"She's a lawyer," Jake said, his heart rate quickening.

"True enough, and it turns out quite a famous one recently in New York City. I got this fax this morning," Carl said, reaching into his suit pocket and pulling out the paper. "Go ahead. Read it. She made *The New York Times* even."

"What kind of game are you playing here, Carl?"

"Go ahead, Jake. If you think it's that crazy, you have nothing to concern yourself with, right?"

Jake grabbed the paper out of Carl's hand and read the headline: "*Terri Lawson, Transgendered Lawyer, Breaks Boundaries in the Law Community.*"

Jake stared at the paper in disbelief. Right next to the headline was a picture of Terri, and the article went on to discuss her *pro bono* work within the transgendered community. Jake's eye zeroed in on the introductory sentence of one paragraph, "*Before I transitioned to a woman, I lived for years feeling alien in my former body – a man's body.*"

"I guess I'll take off now since I got you updated, cuz. You can thank me later once you process all this. Just thought you'd want to know that *she* used to be a *he*. Y'all have a good morning now," said Carl smugly. And with that, he turned around and walked back to his car.

Jake just stood in the doorway motionless, his mind going a million miles a minute. A burnt smell began to permeate from the kitchen through the wide open door. As Carl drove off down the driveway, Jake looked upstairs, thinking of Terri.

As Carl headed down the highway, he smiled widely. This had been a good morning alright. He had never dreamed he would hit this kind of pay dirt. This Lawson character would no doubt run straight out of town now that her, or his, secret was out. Carl didn't understand what any of this transgendered stuff really meant, but he knew his old-fashioned cousin wouldn't be for it. Once word spread throughout town, and Carl would make sure it would, this Terri Lawson would probably want to head straight back to the city on the first flight out of Billings.

And if she didn't, the next phase of Carl's plan surely would drive her out and get her to sell him that damned land. Everything was falling into place.

Terri woke up feeling the warmth of the sunlight on her face. She leisurely stretched, and instinctively reached out for Jake. Upon realizing he wasn't there, she opened her eyes and found the space next to her in the bed empty. Had he already gotten up before her? The smell of something burnt in the air awakened her senses.

She reached for her robe and headed down the stairs.

He certainly wouldn't have left without waking her, would he? Maybe he had an emergency. He was the sheriff after all. Perhaps he just didn't want to wake her.

She followed the smell of the overcooked food and was surprised to see a skillet with burnt sausages in it. The coffee container had been taken out of the fridge, but a pot hadn't been brewed.

"Jake?" she called out. "Are you here?"

Why would he start cooking food and suddenly leave?

She walked into the living room, and a piece of paper sitting on the coffee table just happened to catch her eye. It appeared to be a fax.

She walked over, picked up the paper, and immediately felt a sense of dread sweep through her being. It was a copy of the newspaper article in *The New York Times*. *The article*. Her article.

"Where did...?" she wondered.

She then noticed at the top of the fax the phone number and the name "Carl Collins" next to it.

She felt tears in her eyes at the realization

of the morning's events. She couldn't believe
this was happening. Feelings of guilt and the all
too familiar hurt filled her heart and mind, as she
sat down on the couch and began to cry. She
cried for Tom breaking up the engagement, for
Uncle Bud's passing, and perhaps her never
seeing Jake again. She messed up the special
connection she felt for Jake, the kind of
connection she thought she would never feel
again. She should have told him beforehand.

What must Jake be thinking? Was he
feeling hurt? Humiliated? Used? Did he even
understand what any of this meant?

She quickly dressed and tried calling Jake
on his cell, but her call went directly to
voicemail.

"Um, hi, Jake. I was just wondering what
happened...? If what I think may have happened
did, I understand if you're confused, but
please....I'd like to talk to you. Please give me a
chance to *try* and explain my situation to you.
Call me. Thanks."

A knock on the door startled her.

"Jake!" she called, hurrying to the door.

However, when she opened the door she
was perplexed to find an elderly Native
American gentleman with long braided white
hair wearing black rimmed glasses. Behind him
were two college aged young men carrying cases
of some sort.

"Uh, may I help you?" Terri asked
perplexed.

"You must be Terri Lawson!" the

gentleman exclaimed and held out his hand to be shook.

She cautiously shook the man's hand and said, "Uh, I am. And you are?"

"I'm Professor Redfeather. Jake Collins, a former student of mine, called me and said you may have some artifacts on your property I may find of interest. I'm head of a local archeology society, and I've brought along a couple of students from the local college to assist. Jake said it would be okay to stop by. I hope we didn't arrive at a bad time."

Terri shook her head, "Of course not. I'm glad to see you and help in any way I can."

She tried to put on her game face, the one she used in the courtroom when she thought she may be losing a case and she didn't want to let on. Here was this nice older man wanting to look through her property right at the moment she felt like her head was spinning.

"Excellent!" Professor Redfeather said, beaming. "Could you guide us where to start? Where you found the pottery shards?"

"Sure," she answered. "Give me just a moment, and I'll be back down."

First, she would get the Professor started, and then she would go into town to try and find Jake. *She had to find Jake.*

Immediately when Terri walked into the diner, she felt all eyes on her. This time it felt different than the first time she came into town.

This time she felt like their eyes gazed at her with harshness and judgment.

She saw Sally at the counter, and Sally breathed what appeared to be a sigh of relief when she saw her. Sally quickly waved her over.

"Mindy, hon, watch the front," Sally said, taking Terri by the hand and leading her into the back.

Terri noticed how Mindy just stared at her looking wide-eyed and amazed.

Once they were in the storage room behind the kitchen, Terri said, "Sally, I need to find Jake. I need to talk to him."

"I figured," she said, nodding. "I'm sure you two have some things discuss."

Terri eyed her suspiciously and said, "What do you know?"

Sally looked at her with sad eyes and said, "Oh, hon, I'm sorry, but everything that happens in a small town spreads faster than a whore's legs at a Nevada brothel. That Carl Collins made some phone calls last night about you from what I understand, and one thing leads to another. Is it true, dear? What they say?"

Terri felt a sinking feeling in the pit of her stomach.

"Does everybody know?" she asked.

Sally nodded.

"I should have talked to Jake first and explained some things to him, but I just...I just didn't think I'd be here long enough for it to matter. Don't get me wrong. I'm proud of who I am. It took me a long time to get to this point in my life, and I had years of struggle. But sometimes you just don't want to have to get into your *story* with every person. You just want to be who you are *now*. Not everyone is open to understanding."

Sally reached out and took her hand and said, "Listen to me, honey. Bud spoke of you like you were the apple of his eye, and I had so much respect for that man. I know you're a good person. I'm not one to judge, either. My sister and her lesbian partner live in Billings, and I love both of them to pieces. I know it's not the same thing as your situation…I guess what I'm trying to tell you is that I'm here for you."

Terri just nodded. She tried to hold back the tears she felt forming in her eyes.

"However, some people here," Sally said, sighing, "are a little closed minded. Mostly it's because they rarely meet anyone that's different from them. All they know is within fifty miles of here."

"I know. I've spent years educating people. It's tiring. It's just sometimes you don't feel like…"

"Having to educate people. I get it," Sally said. She paused for a moment, and she appeared to be forming her next words carefully. "Jake is a good man, a real good man. He doesn't open his heart easily because…"

"His fiancée died. He told me last night." Terri finished.

Sally nodded and continued, "And he's probably never encountered a woman… like you.

You have to give him some time to think about this. Talk to him."

"I know. I should have told him before...I made a terrible mistake," Terri said, her eyes locking with Sally's.

A look of understanding flashed across Sally's face, and Terri knew that she understood what the *before* referred to.

"You were intimate," Sally said.

"Yeah," Terri admitted. "It just all happened so fast."

Sally squeezed her hand and said, "You might need to give Jake some time, but don't give up."

"I won't. I can't. I need to make him understand why I didn't tell him before *and* let him know how special I think he is. I can't leave it like this."

Terri drove by the sheriff's station on the way back to the ranch, but Jake's patrol car and Jeep was nowhere in sight. She continued driving back to the ranch. She went back and forth between feeling like she should give him some time and talking to him immediately.

When she got back to the ranch, Professor Redfeather and his team were already covered in dirt and sweat.

The old man practically ran to her car when he saw her.

Terri got out and said, "Did you find more?"

"You won't believe what we found, Miss Lawson. I'm going to contact state and federal authorities. You might be on top of a major Native American archaeological site."

He held out a piece of earth colored pottery with swipes of blue coloring, a bowl, amazingly intact.

"Look at this piece," the professor said, looking like he was in heaven. She could see why Jake spoke of the professor so fondly. His enthusiasm for the subject was infectious and he had an avuncular quality that reminded her of Bud. "It's in practically flawless condition."

"It is beautiful," Terri said. At least something positive may have come from her trip to Montana.

"Come see, my dear," he said, grabbing her hand and leading her over to a blanket where a few other pieces had been carefully laid out, numbered and photographed.

"You found all of this already?" she said in amazement.

"I know! It's unbelievable, but the tornado managed to unearth things that have been buried for who knows how long. I can't wait until we can start dating some of these pieces."

"What tribe do you think they're from?"

"For this area, most definitely from the Crow I would wager."

Crow. She remembered Jake sharing his heritage with her just the night before when everything had felt so perfect, so right.

"Look at this beauty," the professor said, reaching down and holding up a broken piece of pottery with red and yellow stripes in some sort of unrecognizable design. "I'm hoping to find the other missing pieces to this one. Studying the two-spirit people, the *boté,* has been a large part of my research."

"The two-spirit people?" Terri asked. She began to remember Uncle Bud mentioning something about them before when she was struggling with her transition.

"Yes, many native groups considered some people to contain the spirit of both male and female. Not really gay or lesbian but a third gender almost. The tribes thought that the individual would decide their gender, not just the physical appearance. It was definitely a different world view than the European settlers."

"Really?" Terri said, fascinated. She definitely felt a connection to what the Professor was telling her. Would she have been considered one of those two-spirits? "What was their place in society? These two-spirit people?"

"It varied from tribe to tribe. Many of them were considered a gift to the tribe though and given special jobs to do, such as healing people. Some were also known for their pottery making. The Crow also considered them very lucky in love. It was not unusual for a male-bodied, female spirit person to marry a male identified tribe member."

"I had no idea," Terri said, dumbstruck. "It sounds so much more advanced than our society now."

The professor nodded knowingly. "When it comes to our society's rigid views regarding sexuality or gender, you're right. It was seen as a positive rather than a negative. Diversity was a reflection of nature and all its infinite possibilities."

"If only it were that way now," Terri said softly.

"Professor, we may have found something else!" one of the assistants called out.

"If you'll excuse me," he said, hurrying back to the site.

"Of course! Take your time, Professor. You have my permission to excavate as much as you need to."

The professor grabbed her hands and shook them excitedly.

"Thank you very much! This is indeed very exciting! I think we're onto something really big!"

"I'll put on some coffee for you and your team," she offered.

"That would be much appreciated," the professor said. "This has been such a lucky find!"

Terri tried numerous times to call Jake, but every time it went straight to voicemail. She prayed he would give her at least a chance to tell him her side of the story. She didn't want to end things this way with so many loose ends.

She spent much of the day watching Professor Redfeather and his team go about their work and fixed them some turkey sandwiches for lunch. The whole time the professor's story about the two-spirits stayed in her mind. What it must have felt like to be so accepted by your fellow tribespeople from the beginning. So different from her own experience. *And supposedly we were the more advanced people bringing civilization to the natives*, Terri thought.

At the end of the day, the professor requested to come back the next day to continue, and Terri agreed.

Compulsively, she checked her phone a few times to see if she may have missed Jake's call. Nothing. He obviously didn't want to speak to her. Feelings of rejection crept into the back of her mind. It was like reliving the break-up with Tom all over again but this time it seemed more painful.

Terri went into the bathroom to look at herself. She washed her face and took off her make-up and stared at the person in the mirror. After years of therapy and a living a life as a woman before her operation, she felt ready-- ready for the surgery and the follow-up hormone treatments. And now, looking at herself, she was finally the woman she always had imagined she would be. When she was Terrence, she fought so hard to make the true her disappear. Now Terri had a career and friends who loved her. And yet instead of having everything, she seemed to be losing everything. Uncle Bud. Tom. And now

Jake. Beautifully handsome and gentlemanly
Jake. How she longed to snuggle into his firm,
smooth chest and be wrapped up by his strong
arms again. Would last night be their only night
together?

Her pondering was interrupted by a loud
crashing sound downstairs and the sound of a
speeding car. She hurried downstairs to find a
rock thrown into her front window, broken glass
littered the living room floor. She rushed to the
door and could only see red taillights fading into
the distance. She ran down the walkway
hysterical, shocked and angry. The day had been
one disaster after another.

"Damn you!" was all she could yell out
of the top of her lungs, the words disappearing
into the empty landscape.

She turned around and could see spray
painted words illuminated by the porch light.
The words "Freak Go Home" in red paint glared
back at her against backdrop of the ranch home.
But the sight didn't sadden Terri, it actually
fueled her anger. How dare they ruin Uncle
Bud's house! She had done nothing to anyone
there to deserve this type of aggression. Were
people here that scared of someone who was
different from them?

Many people would back down, but not
Terri. She had learned many years ago that
giving in accomplished nothing.

She took a deep breath, tried to calm
herself and her now shaky nerves. She went into
the house and called 911. The dispatcher said

someone would come over. She couldn't help but wonder if that person would be Jake. Please let it be Jake. She wanted, needed, to see him one more time.

       Back in town, Carl handed out the last of the $20 bills into the hands of two kids. "You sure the person in the house didn't see you?"

       "Nah, man, we parked far away and drove off before anyone could see us," the pierced and tattooed teen named Gus said, looking smug.

       "I saw that thing running out the door behind us though! We got that house good man!" the other boy, this one more scrappy with red hair, nicknamed Carrot said.

       "Good work," Carl said. "Now, make sure you don't breathe a word of this to no one. Don't go bragging to your buddies. That's how people get caught. Understand?"

       "Yeah, yeah, we got you," Gus said.

       Carl walked off with a wide smile of satisfaction on his face. He lit up a cigarette and took a long, slow drag, feeling more relaxed and confident than he ever had been in a long time.

Chapter 11

Terri ran outside in the moonlight when she saw the blue and red flashing lights approaching. She felt a lump in her throat when she saw Jake climb out of the patrol car. He looked down at the gravel as he approached her. She wanted to hug him and have him comfort her, but his body language indicated otherwise.

"Jake!" she said. "I wondered if you'd be the one to come out."

He finally looked up, and his eyes met hers for a brief second before he surveyed the damage.

"I'm the only one who *could* come out right now," he admitted.

She felt a twinge of disappointment. She had wanted him to come out to make sure she was okay, protected, just like after the storm.

He walked towards the house, and his eyes mentally took notes.

"I'm sorry about this. Some people truly are despicable," he said.

She wondered if he meant only the vandals or was she included in that statement.

"How long ago?" he asked, taking a pen and pad out of his pocket.

"About ten minutes ago. The rock came crashing through the window. All I saw when I came out was red taillights. When I turned around, I found this," she said motioning to the hate graffiti that now covered the front of Uncle Bud's house, now her house.

"Let me look things over," Jake said, his voice void of emotion. "Show me where the rock is."

They walked up on the porch and started to go inside but Jake paused.

"Terri, aren't you going to say something?" Jake blurted out as he stood behind her.

A moment passed and Terri took a deep breath to steel herself before she turned around to face Jake. He looked even more handsome tonight than when she last saw him. The emotions she felt being near him began to pour into her once again.

When her eyes met his, he could have sworn he felt his heartbeat increase ten-fold. The whole day his mind had been reeling from what Carl told him. He tried to make sense of it. He'd never known a woman like her before, and yet, while making love to her the night before he never noticed any difference. He had used protection, but she looked, sounded, felt and even tasted like a woman to him. He tried to reconcile the two in his mind.

He felt confused and betrayed. How could she not tell him such an important piece of information? Didn't he deserve as much? Jake had always considered himself a man who didn't care what others thought of him. So, it pained him to admit to himself that he hated the looks and stares from the other townspeople all day.

Talking behind his back. If it were true, what did that make him? He could see them whispering, the sideways glances, and the smirks.

"Your cousin, Carl, spoke to you didn't he?" she said at last. She averted her eyes as if it pained her to look at him. "You know, don't you?"

"I do," Jake said, holding his uniform hat by his side and trying to keep his composure. He tried to go into "sheriff mode," to not let his feelings get the best of him. Instead, he would question the "witness" and get answers to his questions. Keep it strictly professional, even though he was vested in this case emotionally as well. To think about it too much on a personal level hurt too badly. She had been the first woman he had felt himself truly opening up to since Sherilynn, and now he was left with nothing but a bunch of questions. "What I want to know is why *you* didn't tell me? You had every chance. Do you know how it felt to have Carl be the one to tell me?"

Jake paused, and he appeared to be struggling for the words to express himself.

"How did it make you feel?" she asked, the words barely escaping her throat.

"Betrayed," he said finally, the words cutting into her heart like a sharp knife into butter. "I don't pretend to understand everything...*yet.* I may be a small town sheriff but didn't you respect me enough to tell the truth? But I would have rather heard it from you first hand. Don't you think I deserved at least that, Terri? Don't you? Didn't I deserve some respect after all we've been through?"

"You do," she admitted. "I don't know how I could have handled anything here without you, Jake. I needed you. I was afraid..."

"Of?"

"What do you mean *of?*" she said, suddenly sounding defensive. "I wanted to tell you last night. After the fair. Before we...made love. You must know how it scared me to tell you. But then I wanted to tell you the next morning...but you were gone. I felt so abandoned."

Her mind transported her back to that magical night when Jake had made her feel exactly how a man should make a woman feel...sexy, loved, and protected.

"I just never thought things would go this far, Jake," she admitted. "And last night happened. It was special to me. I don't know how you feel but I'll always remember it..."

"Well, the jury's still out," he said, leaning back on the porch post and gazing at the sky as if searching for answers. "I'm not sure where all this is going. But here we are."

She took a deep breath and asked the one question she feared knowing the answer to the most, "Does knowing everything change the way you feel?"

He turned to face her, and Terri searched his countenance for the answer. Jake's mind went back to the night before, the kisses, the caresses, the feeling of a true connection when he made love to her. How could he not have known, sensed a difference? Was he different now? He had so many questions swirling in his mind.

"You should have told me," Jake said exasperated and challenging her. "I thought I knew you. Who are you Terri?"

Terri grabbed a lock of her hair with both her hands and closed her eyes, gathering her thoughts. How do you explain the years of growing up hating your body? Feeling it was alien to the person inside? Or all the years seeing other friends mature into young women while your voice was getting deeper, facial hair was growing, and instead of your womanhood below, something else was developing? It felt like a constant struggle to keep having to explain who she was to so many people. Why couldn't people just accept her as the woman she now was? How could she explain it to Jake, who she cared for so deeply, yet she was afraid he would hurt her like her ex?

Terri inhaled sharply and began to tell the truth. "That boy that I was then, that people saw… I had to get rid of him because I had no choice, or I felt like I would die." "I don't understand any of this. How can you say you didn't have a choice to go from being a man to a woman?" Jake retorted.

Terri fought back the tears as the floodgates of her memories were rushing back in. "I had no choice. I knew when I was little that I was in the wrong body. It was one of my earliest memories when I was five. I prayed to God that when puberty hit I would start to change. And I did change. I became less and less what I felt inside. And when I was finally brave enough to do it while in law school, my new life began. I became who I was always meant to be..."

Jake looked at her sympathetically. He appeared to be *trying* to understand her, and that, to Terri, demonstrated just how good of a man he was. She could imagine most of the men from this small town freaking out completely, treating her like a pariah, painting this horrible graffiti on Uncle Bud's house, but yet here he was at least asking her the questions. Trying to bridge the gap.

"Some people, such as most of my family, couldn't accept my transitioning. They called me a monster and cut all ties with me. You wouldn't understand what that's like. Being different. Look at you. You're perfect. You've never felt like a...like a...a freak," she said accusingly. Her tears started to flow, and she turned away from Jake.

Jake shoved his hands in his pockets and sighed deeply. *Freak.* Jake hated that word and any word that made people feel less than. He remembered being on the school playground in elementary school and having the other kids call him half-breed. It made him hate his native heritage at the time, and now that shamed him. It was only when he took Professor Redfeather's class did he realize the wisdom of the first peoples, living in harmony with the land and their many accomplishments. He understood being different and the cruelty of others. He felt his experience gave him the empathy he needed to be a good person as well as a good sheriff. He looked at her now, so vulnerable. He couldn't help but think that she was still so beautiful.

"Let's go in and survey the damage. Where did the rock land exactly?" Jake asked, abruptly changing the subject as his mind continued to try to sort everything.

She watched him walk inside the house, and she tried in vain to fight back the tears. Was that it? Did he not want to hear her anymore? The feelings of last night rushed into her brain, and she yearned for his warm, comforting embrace. Jake had made her feel wanted again, and it had scared and enthralled Terri at the same time. But just as quickly as it happened between them, it had fallen apart.

She walked into the house and found him crouched down and examining the rock and the damage. He shook his head in disgust.

"I'm sorry about this," he said softly, removing his examining gloves.

She shrugged and said, "It's not your fault."

Jake stood back up and said, "You know you can't stay here tonight."

"What?" she said in surprise. As shaken as she was, she'd never been one to run especially since transitioning. She had spent far too many years running from things and didn't want to do it anymore. Terri was tired of being afraid and this latest occurrence only strengthened her resolve.

"It's not safe here for you tonight. What if the vandals come back? What if they have other plans...?"

"I'm not going anywhere. Those bigots are running me away from my own house."

Jake moaned in exasperation and ran his hand through his thick, dark hair. "Please, don't be stubborn about this. Take my advice. What would you do if they came back and tried to do something worse than spray painting or throwing rocks?"

She pondered the thought and fear began to creep into her mind. Yet, she just hated the idea of having these close-minded people run her off with her tail between her legs.

"I can take care of myself," she said, but she knew her voice now betrayed her. She sounded concerned and worried.

Jake was silent for a moment. His eyes scanned the room. They looked anywhere but at her directly. Eventually, he said, "Fine. But I'm staying here with you."

"Oh," was all she could manage to say.

"On the couch," he quickly added. "If they see the patrol car and a light on, they won't try and do anything. I'm sure."

"You don't have to do this," she said.

"I took an oath," Jake replied, finally looking her in the eye. "To protect and to serve *all* the citizens of my county, and I meant that."

God, she had dreamed for so long to find a man with this kind of integrity. She realized that deep down she had already known Tom was not that kind of man, but she refused to see it. She had so wanted to be loved and accepted for the woman she was, so wanted the dream, and it kept her from seeing what was right in front of her.

The two of them spent the next few minutes in awkward silence while Terri gathered up some extra sheets and pillows from the linen closet.

She started to make up the couch, but he waved her away saying, "It's okay. Let me do it." He promptly took the beddings from her, their hands briefly touching.

Not knowing how far to press him on anything now, she stepped back. "Are you sure?"

"Yep," he said, spreading the sheet. "This'll be fine. Compared to a night out camping in the mountains, this is a five star hotel."

She noticed that he was still dressed in his full uniform though, striking a handsome pose.

"Thanks again for staying tonight."

He nodded and said, "In the morning, we'll figure out what to do next."

They stood there for a moment in silence again. Only the sound of their breathing permeated the room. Not a word was said, but there was a deafening cacophony of emotion in their minds.

"Good night," Terri said, heading for the stairs.

"Night," Jake called after her as he turned out the lights.

It took a while, but, eventually, Terri fell into a fitful sleep. The ringing of her cell phone had awakened her from a vivid dream where she was running around the lake surrounding the ranch. In the dream, she was searching frantically for something, but she couldn't recall what it was she was trying to find. She was afraid of looking into the water lest that reflection of him—of Terrence—would appear again.

She thought she would let the phone go to voicemail, but it just rang again and again. She reached over to the nightstand, picked it up, and saw the number was Martin's office.

"Hey, Martin," she said, still feeling groggy and trying to sit up.

"I woke you up," Martin said on the other end of the line, sounding tense. "I forgot about the time difference."

"It's okay. What's going on? You sound so serious. I needed to get up anyways," she wondered if Jake was still downstairs. Was he waiting on her to get up?

"I hated to call you, Terri. I know you're

trying to sort things out, but…"

"It's okay. What's going on?"

"Hanson insisted that I call you. He's freaking out."

John Hanson was one of the senior partners at the firm she worked for, and Terri knew him to always be a calm and collected man. For him to be upset, it must be something big.

"What's going on?"

"The clients on the McBriar case are upset with the direction of the proceedings with their new copyright infringement suit. They're threatening to walk and go to another firm unless you come back pronto to take the case over," Martin answered.

McBriar Inc. had been one of her firm's biggest clients for two decades and a leading software designer in the computer industry. The CEO had always been a bear to handle, but for some reason, Terri always had had the magic touch with dealing with him.

"I know you need your time off, and I hate to ask you to do this, but…" Martin started to say.

"Don't worry. I'll head back on the earliest flight to New York," she answered firmly.

"Are you sure? I know you've got a lot of *stuff* to deal with right now."

"I'm very sure, Martin. If I can save this client relationship, I'm going to. For you. For Hanson. For the firm."

"Thanks so much, Terri. If anyone can save it, it's you."

"I'll call you when I'm at the airport. Besides, I think I might have overstayed my welcome in Montana," she said.

"Huh, what do you mean? Did you have a run-in with the law and are getting run out of Dodge?" he joked, not realizing how accurate he was.

"Martin, as usual, you are uncanny," she replied. "I'll tell you all the dirt when I get back. Make sure my favorite coffee is brewing..."

After hanging up with Martin, she crawled out of the bed and went into the bathroom to wash her face and brush her teeth. How was she going to leave everything that needed to be done here, too? She had the clean-up, the excavation, not to mention wanting to right things with Jake.

She heard voices coming from outside her window, and when she walked over she looked down in the yard to see Jake talking to Professor Redfeather, who had already returned with his team for another day of digging. The two men looked pleased to see each other as they shook hands and chatted.

So much had been started here and left unfinished. Terri had *made* herself the type to finish things. The thought of whether she was using this business emergency as an excuse entered her mind, but she realized that she did have to go. John Hanson, along with the other partners, had more than given her a few opportunities, and she owed it to him and the firm. Plus, she still had bills to pay, and her job, the career she had so fought for, was important to her. Terri discovered when you are indecisive, sometimes life makes the decisions for you.

After a quick shower and dressing in a pair of jeans and sleeveless light blue blouse, she headed downstairs, looked through the window, and saw Jake standing on the porch watching the professor and his team head out to a plot of land behind the house.

She gathered her courage to face him again and walked outside to stand next to him.

"Good morning," she said cheerfully.

"Morning," he said, giving her a quick glimpse.

She could have sworn she saw hurt *and* desire in his eyes.

"Professor Redfeather was asking about the graffiti," Jake said. "He was very concerned for you."

"You can tell him what happened. You can tell him *everything*. I have nothing to hide."

She immediately regretted those last words since she had hid something from Jake, something big, and she knew it.

"I had some more officers come out. They're questioning the neighbors down the road to see if they saw or heard anything."

"Thank you," she replied. "And thanks

again for staying last night."

"No problem," he said, looking at her again but this time keeping his gaze fixed on her.

She wondered if he was as conflicted as she was. She thought he looked torn between wanting to turn away again or to kiss her. God, how she wished he would grab her up in his arms again. She wanted to feel his body pressed against hers again more than anything. But she was also rationalizing in her mind that what happened that night might have been the last.

"Jake, I…umm…I have to leave to go back to New York."

He looked stunned for a moment before saying quietly, "When?"

"On the first flight I can get out of Billings."

"You're running away?"

"I'm *not* running away," she said, wishing she hadn't sounded so defensive just then. "I just got a call. It's work. There's an emergency. A lot of money is involved, and they seem to think I'm the only one who can handle the situation. I'm not sure how long it will take, and there's so much going on here with the dig, the house and with…"

Her voice trailed off. She wanted to say so much going on with *us*. But she didn't know if she and Jake had any semblance of an *us* now.

"I want the professor to continue his work though, but I'm worried about the house," she said.

"I'll stay here for a while," Jake replied.

"I know a good painter who'll take care of the graffiti for you. I'll keep an eye out on things."

"I can't ask you to do that," Terri said.

"You didn't ask me. I volunteered. Look, Bud did a lot for me when I was just a teen. Sometimes he was the only father figure I had. So, I want to watch over things for him…and you. It's the least I can do."

Terri felt an overwhelming sense of gratitude, but before she could tell Jake, a cry came from the distance. It was the Professor.

"Jake! Come see this!" they both heard the professor call out excitedly.

"Be there in two shakes of a lamb's tail, Professor!" Jake called back, before turning back to Terri and said, "Let me go see what he's found now. He's very excited so far."

"I guess I should go start packing," she said about to turn away from the man who awakened deep emotions within her. She felt the moment was bittersweet.

He looked like he was about to say something, but then he just nodded and walked down the steps and towards Professor Redfeather.

She watched him for a moment, his masculine figure walking away from her, possibly forever. Terri wished so badly that things could have been different. She was speeding into town upon her arrival and now her departure left her with a slow, aching feeling inside.

Chapter 12

Four months later.

"Terri?"

The sound of her name snapped her back to reality as she had been staring out her skyscraper office window watching all the people on the street below running around like worker ants. She loved the energy of New York City--the way that it felt like anything could happen anytime and the possibilities were endless. And yet, she also missed the quiet vastness of the Montana landscape. Her two worlds. Apparently irreconcilable.

"Martin," she said, turning around. "I'm sorry. I didn't hear you walking in. I guess I was lost in my thoughts."

"I bet!" Martin exclaimed, walking in and smiling from ear to ear. "Trying to figure out how you pulled off that miracle in the courtroom today? What are you going to do for an encore, lady? Walk on water? That was pure genius today."

Upon returning to New York, Terri had convinced McBriar Inc. not to bolt on their firm, and she ultimately, after many long weeks, won their case for them.

"Thanks, Martin," she replied. "That was a tough one."

"A tough one, but you did it. I knew you

would though. Want to go grab drinks tonight with the rest of the team to celebrate?"

Normally, Terri would automatically say yes as the celebratory drinks after a hard case won was practically mandatory, but she had allowed herself to be so consumed with the work that she never let herself emotionally deal with all she left behind in her short time in Montana.

"Would it be okay if I just headed home? I'm not feeling well."

"It wouldn't be the same without the star lawyer! Hope nothing too bad," Martin said concerned.

"Nah. I'll be fine."

"You still thinking of Montana? The ranch? Of Jake?" Martin inquired. She had confided in him upon her return and always, he was the eternal optimist.

"You know me too, well, Martin. Am I that transparent?"

"I just know you. That's all. Well, rain check on the drinks then. I'll give everyone your regrets."

"Thanks, Martin. I think I just need time alone tonight."

"Of course. But before I go, remember that talk we had before you left for Montana?"

"Yes, you talked about the important things in life," Terri recalled.

"Well, good work has its place. But don't forget that love is what binds it all together. There'd be no one to share things with. Without love, what's the point?" he said with eyebrows

raised while closing her office door quietly
behind him.

Once she got back to her apartment in
Greenwich Village, she poured herself a glass of
Chardonnay, and sat on her balcony to relax
watching the sun set over the vibrant city and the
skyscrapers lighting up horizon. Just that
morning before heading into the courtroom she
had gotten a call from Professor Redfeather.

In the time since she left Montana and
after some deep thinking, she did something she
thought would please Uncle Bud. She donated
the entire ranch to Professor Redfeather's
organization so that further study and
preservation would be done. The professor had
been thrilled and insisted that they would leave
the ranch house on the property, and Terri would
be able to stay there any time she felt like it.
He'd have that stipulation drawn up in the
papers.

Terri thought about Jake often while
working or at home alone. She hadn't spoken to
him since she left, but she learned through the
professor that Jake would stay on at the ranch
until the property transfer to watch over things
for her.

So many nights, she wanted to pick up
the phone and call him and try to talk things out.
But she was ashamed to admit that fear kept her
from doing so. What if he simply didn't want to
talk about it? He never tried to call her. And

why would he? After all, she had left him behind in Montana to deal with everything: the excavation at the ranch and especially the town learning her about her secret. She had abandoned him and wouldn't be surprised if he didn't want to see her again. Terri felt she had no compelling reason to go back to Montana even though her heart ached to see Jake again.

But to her surprise, Professor Redfeather called later that night and said, "You must simply come for the dedication ceremony, Miss Lawson. It would mean so much to all of us to thank you in person for your generosity."

She was excited about the professor's plans to turn the land into a research center and, ultimately, a museum that could draw visitors to Clearview. It was a win-win situation for all. Now that the site had been also legally given historical preservation status, it was protected from Carl and his condo project development. She knew the outcome would have made her Uncle Bud so happy if he were alive. But the fear of facing Jake and what he may *or may not* say haunted her as soon as she hung up the phone with the professor.

But then she remembered how Uncle Bud used to always tell her, "Don't ever be afraid to be happy. *Ever.* Life is too short."

She finished her glass of wine in one large gulp, a little liquid courage, and walked back in the apartment to go online and book a plane ticket to back to Billings, Montana.

***

Driving in her rental car back onto the ranch for the first time in months, Terri was amazed at the transformation. All of the mess from the tornado had been cleaned. The ranch had been freshly painted and that horrible graffiti covered over and wiped away. A sign at the beginning of the driveway announced that she had arrived to the "Clearview First Peoples Research and Study Center."

When she pulled up, Professor Redfeather excitedly ran outside to greet her. He embraced her warmly and said, "I'm so pleased you're here for the dedication ceremony, Miss Lawson. We have one of the bedrooms all fixed up for you."

"That's so sweet. Thank you," Terri said.

As happy as she was with how things had turned out for the ranch, she still felt a twinge of sadness that Uncle Bud's presence was no longer the predominant one here. And she still had all of his personal belongings which had been placed in storage to go through.

The professor insisted on carrying her luggage inside and noticed Terri hesitant to go in.

"Would you mind if I spent a few moments walking around the grounds, Professor?" she asked, feeling the need to have a few moments to herself with all the feelings and memories rushing into her mind.

"Of course. Please take your time. Without you this would not have been at all possible. When you're ready I'll be inside with a fresh pot of coffee. I can show you some more of the exciting items we've discovered here on the land."

"Thank you," she said. She looked around the landscape surrounding her and remembered how beautiful and peaceful it had been. So different from the dark, cramped, and noisy city. She could be alone with her thoughts as she headed towards the lake on the trail Jake had once shown her.

Finally, she approached the water's edge and took in a deep breath of the clean country air. She hadn't realized how much she had missed the crisp smell along with the serene quietness on the water and on the land, much of it still untouched and unspoiled.

"Terri," she heard a familiar voice say behind her. Startled, she jumped and when she started to turn around she lost her footing and was falling towards the lake's surface. But once again a pair of strong, masculine hands reached out and grabbed her. *Jake.*

Jake pulled her up and back towards the land and towards him.

"I'm beginning to think that you want to fall into that lake," he said jokingly.

"And what would I do if you weren't here to catch me?" she said, stepping back a short distance and looking at him again.

God, if it was even possible, he looked even more handsome and strong in his uniform than before. His face seemed softened since their last words together.

"You look...great. I heard you were arriving today," he said. "I wanted to..."

He paused as they stared at one another. They seemed to lose track of time gazing into each other's eyes. She felt a cool breeze come over the lake, and then rays of sunshine broke through a cloud, practically spotlighting the two of them by the lake.

"I wanted to let you know we found out who attacked your house that night."

She couldn't help but feel a moment of disappointment. While she wanted the vandals to be caught, they weren't the words she cared to hear. She wanted Jake to *want* her again.

"A kid, just turned seventeen, came into the station this morning, believe it or not. He said he had found Jesus and had to confess. Said that Carl paid him and another kid to do it."

"Carl! Why that no good son of a..." Terri said. The lengths that man went to just to close a real estate deal made some of the biggest sharks she met in New York City seem like minnows in comparison.

"My sentiments exactly. It makes me sick to know a member of my family would do something like that," Jake said. "I'm going to make sure he gets sentenced and punished for what he did. And word will spread how he likes to conduct business around here. His reputation's good as gone."

Terri stood quiet for a moment, and then shook her head, looking at a small flower at her feet growing by the lake.

"Don't. I'm not going to press charges if that's what's needed."

"What? Why?" Jake said perplexed.

Terri reached down and plucked the purple wild flower that grew by the water. The simple yet beautiful nature of this place still amazed her. Life goes on, wherever it is.

"He has a family to support. What will his wife and children do without him? I'll be the bigger person here."

"Wow, you amaze me," Jake said. "You don't have to do that for him, you know? He can get what's coming to him."

"I know," she said, before adding, "Instead tell him I won't press charges *if* he makes a sizeable donation to the new research center."

Jake smiled. "I think that sounds like a plan. I bet you are good in the courtroom, Miss Lawson."

She looked down at the delicate flower, as delicate as her heart felt. She needed to say what ached within her soul. *Don't ever be scared to be happy,* Uncle Bud's words echoed in her head. Even if this situation didn't *or couldn't* go the way she would ultimately like, she had to get things off her chest and make peace with herself.

"I thought about calling you all the time, Jake. Every day I thought about it. I wanted to try and at least help you understand why I did what I did. And I wanted to tell you how much you meant to me. I honestly don't know how I could have made it through the things that happened here without you."

"Thank you for your kindness. I've had a lot of time to think, and actually, Professor Redfeather has helped me."

"He has? In what way?" Terri asked.

"We've talked a lot about his research of the two-spirit people and the special roles they played within the tribe. But, I already knew you were...are...special. I just didn't realize how special you were until you left. I missed you," he paused before adding, "I did think about calling you."

Terri's heart swelled with happiness at those words. It hadn't been only her who felt the pain of their separation. He had been thinking about her, too.

"Look, I know that you live in the big city, and I'm just a country guy that may not understand everything about you...*yet*," Jake said, weighing his words carefully. He wondered if she knew how much courage it took him to open his heart up just a little again. Here he was a man who faced criminals and the unknown every day, but matters of the heart, and the idea of being hurt and losing love again, terrified him. "But maybe while you're here in town we could have dinner. Sally wants to see you at the Café. We can talk some things out some and get reacquainted. Start all over without any secrets."

"Deal," Terri said. "Dinner sounds delightful. Under one condition."

"Uh, oh! What's that?" Jake said, looking at her mischievous eyes.

"No Viking-on-a-Stick. I loved it, but a gal has to watch her figure. Two spirits, okay. Two bodies, not so much."

Jake chuckled and his eyes sparkled the way they did the day they went to the MontanaFair.

"Deal," he said.

And then, catching her by surprise, Jake reached out and took her hand. She had forgotten how nice and warm he felt. His hand was strong yet gentle, like Sheriff Jake Collins himself.

"Want to head back? I know Professor Redfeather is very excited to show you some of his discoveries," Jake cocked his head toward the ranch house.

She squeezed his hand, smiled, and said, "That'd be wonderful, Jake. I'd love to go back."

The two of them headed towards the house, hand in hand, the future unclear but still full of possibilities, like the endless autumn Montana sky.

Also available…

Success had always come easy to the dashing corporate CEO, Maxwell Van Buren. But when the restaurant chain inspired by his great-grandfather's taco cart begins to falter in a tough economy, Max makes it his personal mission to covertly discover the secrets of a few thriving mom-and-pop restaurants in the desert Southwest and use those ideas to save the family business.

Stranded on a sweltering Arizona roadside, Max is rescued by the gorgeous, independent, and sometime tow-truck driver, Allie. For several years her life has been devoted to raising her young son, running a very successful, if tiny, restaurant, and dodging the occasional romantic overture. When she offers the seemingly down-on-his-luck traveler a temporary job and a place to stay, she may not want to resist opening her heart for much longer.

Max, the long-time city dweller, is taken in by the charms of a simpler lifestyle, and begins to long for the kind of happy, stable family life that he's never really had. But what will Allie think when she finds out who he really is and why he's in Primrose, Arizona in the first place? Can Max revive his family's legacy and win Allie's heart at the same time?

Also includes a bonus read of the first chapter of Madison Martin's new romance novel, Toying With Temptation.

Available from most online book and e-book retailers.